THE MOST HATED
VILLAIN EVER

AND THEY CALL ME God

T. STYLES

NATIONAL BEST SELLING AUTHOR OF *RAUNCHY*

ARE YOU ON OUR EMAIL LIST?
SIGN UP ON OUR WEBSITE
www.thecartelpublications.com
OR TEXT THE WORD: CARTELBOOKS
TO 22828
FOR PRIZES, CONTESTS, ETC.

And They Call Me God

By T. Styles

3

And They Call Me God
By T. Styles

Library of Congress Control Number: 2015935623

ISBN 10: 0996099212

ISBN 13: 978-0996099219

Cover Design: Davida Baldwin www.oddballdsgn.com
www.thecartelpublications.com
First Edition
Printed in the United States of America

By T. Styles   5

What's Up Fam,

I'ma do a little something different in this letter and just get right down to it. "And They Call Me God" is a story of what can happen when selfishness and hate give birth and set their creation free with no love. I promise by the end of this one, you will be left with your jaw hanging, so get ready!

Keeping in line with tradition, we want to give respect to a vet or trailblazer paving the way. With that said we would like to recognize:

David Simon

David Simon is a former journalist and screenwriter for several different mini series and TV shows including one of my favorites, *The Wire. The Wire,* has been named one of the best TV dramas of all time by many critics. Thank you David Simon for giving the world *The Wire*. We are forever changed for having that program. If you have not yet seen it, please update your self.

Aight, Get to it. I'll catch you in the next novel.

Be Easy!

Charisse "C. Wash" Washington
Vice President
The Cartel Publications
www.thecartelpublications.com
www.facebook.com/publishercwash
Instagram: publishercwash
www.twitter.com/cartelbooks

Dedications

I dedicate this novel to all my Twisted Babies!

And They Call Me God

#AndTheyCallMeGod

By T. Styles

"The Ego. Man's gift. Man's curse."
- T. Styles

And They Call Me God

PRESENT DAY

You didn't need to speculate if Samantha Herrnstein was wearing panties as she sashayed up the block—a cigarette crossed between her dirty fingers. Just one glance in her direction and you'd see it all.

A tiny black Chanel purse with a gold chain dangled from her arm; a little past the red mini she wore which failed to hide enough of her bushy box to be considered real clothing. On her back, a guitar case sat, and she hummed a tune from her favorite song.

She had somewhere to be — her Life, her everything summoned and as always she came running.

When she made it up the church's steps, she dropped the cigarette, grinded it with her run over silver pump and pulled open two large black doors before she disappeared inside.

She smiled when she saw her progeny although they hadn't noticed she entered. Their attention was glued on Devonte as he stood behind the pulpit as if ordained. A gold chain with the word God dipped in diamonds dangled from his neck and his eyes were concealed with a pair of dark shades.

As Samantha made it deeper inside something felt eerie. He didn't seem like his usual charismatic self and she sensed danger was imminent.

Splattered dried blood drops dressed Samantha Herrnstein's face, as she switched inside a small interrogation room within the Bladensburg Police Department. Although the crime occurred in Baltimore Maryland, about fifty miles from their current location, The Baltimore Police officers wanted to interview her away from their department, for fear of the investigation being leaked.

Samantha's expression was benumbed and out of place, considering the tragedy she witnessed just an hour earlier. Her tight red mini skirt rose into the crease of her hips, revealing her pink center each time her pale white legs extended forward. An unlit cigarette rested between her fingers as she flopped down bare ass into the wooden seat. She tossed her purse on the table, and elected to sit the guitar case on the floor next to her chair.

Two police officers, June Cash, a beautiful white woman, with large green eyes and Heidi Bryant, a equally stunning black female, with an innocent face that hid her extreme intelligence, strolled behind her, eager to get down to business.

Once inside, June and Heidi leaned against the wall and looked down at Samantha. Both removed a small notepad and pen from their shirt pocket to take notes.

"I didn't see this coming," Samantha said looking at them. "But…we all aren't who we claim to be right?" she paused. "Anyway, the man in the car said I could smoke once I got here." She looked between them. "Either of you model types have a light?"

Not feeling her bullshit, Heidi walked toward the table sitting in front of her. She pulled out the chair and sat down. "I'm not fucking around! How many people, Samantha?"

She frowned and wiggled her cigarette, reminding the women of her question. "Soooooooo I can't smoke?" she asked sarcastically.

June peeled herself off the wall, dipped into her tight jean pockets and lit the cigarette. Once the tip turned orange with fire, Samantha pulled deeply, closed her lids, and allowed the smoke into each crevice of her lungs. Then, and only then did she open her eyes and expel the powder like clouds. "Eighty-five," she said calmly. "Some men…some women…but *all* dead."

Heidi looked at her partner and then back at Samantha, both continued to take notes on her story. "Do you know how this started?" June questioned, the anticipation eating at her core.

Samantha lowered her head, the orange tip chewed at the top of the cigarette, threatening to reduce its length. "I don't have much information…just a little. From our earlier days together. But only he knows how it truly started."

"You have to know something," Heidi said.

"I know how I got involved but how his depravity came to be is anyone's guess," she shrugged.

"In your opinion, what kind of man was he?" Heidi continued.

Samantha's face lit like the New York City skyline at night. Smiling widely as she gazed into her eyes she said, "Thank you."

Confused, Heidi responded, "For what?"

"For giving me enough respect to ask. Before getting here, every detective looked at me as if I were some dumb whore. And maybe I am. But they never thought it was possible that I could articulate the make up of a man who could do such irrevocable acts. But who better than his bitch, someone who has dedicated her life to him, to explain?" She pulled on the cigarette.

June sat down next to her partner. "So what kind of man was he?" June repeated.

By T. Styles   13

Excitedly she said, "Brilliant. Inspiring. Charming." Her mood suddenly dipped. "And evil." Her eyes rolled wildly between them. "The most evil you could imagine. And I love him. *Still.*"

And They Call Me God

PART ONE

CHAPTER ONE
PUSH
Winter – January 1980
Baltimore, Maryland

Inside a small bedroom, within an old raggedy square box house, Angela Lloyd, stood on her knees between her sister, Cindy's brown thighs, and did her best to facilitate the birth of her nephew. Although they could've called 911 for assistance, they couldn't risk the other residents in the house finding out. You see, Cindy wasn't supposed to be pregnant.

"Push, little sis," Angela coached while she placed her cool hands on her sister's warm knees. The loose ponytail that hung down her back was within seconds from unraveling. "I can see him but you gotta push harder."

Cindy raised her head and looked down at her sister. "Is he okay, Angie? Is he alive? I ain't been eating right and—"

"Now ain't the time to come down on yourself because of your drinking and drugging," she said cutting her off. "Plus I ain't got no crystal ball to answer your questions either! Just push this little nigga out so we can figure out everything else. Besides, I've seen your pussy more than I want to."

Cindy forced out a laugh although she was in excruciating pain and the situation caused for anything except humor.

Cindy and Angela lived in *Myers Home For Veteran Families and Children,* in Baltimore for most of their lives. Cindy, sixteen and Angela seventeen, stayed there so long they didn't know anything else.

There was no picture perfect life for these girls. Their lives started harshly when their mother Jennifer served in Vietnam and was murdered on duty, leaving them in the care of their father Albert, who went mad after her death. Not being able to deal with life, he placed a gun to his head and took an early ticket to meet his dearly departed wife in the afterlife.

The children, who were homeless, were given over to Maryland Child Care Services. Since they experienced the tragedy of losing both parents, and wanted to stay together, there was only one option. But it wasn't given to them without warning.

"This place is dangerous girls," Moraine warned as she twisted the wedding ring on her finger. Her eyes moved over one sister and then the other. "I don't feel safe leaving you here but you don't want to be separated," she continued, as she sat in the car outside of Myer's House. "My only question to you is are you sure about this? I can find way better places for you ladies."

Angela looked at Cindy and answered quickly. "We're sure. Please don't separate us, Mrs. Moraine," Angela pleaded, her heart wept inside with the mere thought of losing her sister. "We will live here no matter how bad and follow the rules. You won't have any trouble from us."

"Okay, but only you two can live here...anybody else and they'll throw you out on the streets," Moraine continued. "That means no company of any sort."

"Nobody but us," Angela said.

Moraine, although afraid, agreed. She knew the home had a history of occupiers with mental illnesses. Unlike some children who were there with one or two parents, the girls would be virtually alone. Moraine would stop by once a week and the home's resident managers would make sure their basic needs were met but that was about it.

With the decision of their future made, Moraine gave them a Bible, a lock for their room's door and she put in a request for a telephone line. Afterwards she visited them weekly, monthly, and then quarterly.

During the period when Moraine's visits became fewer and fewer, Cindy met Eugene Harrington, on the way home from school one day. He was a local dude with an erratic behavior and flighty beliefs about life. Before long he convinced her that he would provide for all of her needs if she followed him through fire.

Bored to death, she agreed.

In return he would take her on inexpensive dates, buy her cheap shoes and dig so deeply into her pussy, he planted his seed, thereby making her pregnant with his child within two months of their first date.

Although he promised to stay around, when her pregnancy started showing he left her to fin for herself, claiming the child was not his, even though she was a virgin before he entered her. And there she was, having a baby in secrecy because if her offspring were discovered she would be exiled.

"I see it," Angela said, her eyes sparkling with specks of hope for his future. "It's almost here!"

Cindy pushed a little harder until the baby slid out into the world, screaming and hollering like he knew what they had planned for him. Angela grabbed the only towel she had in the room, which she also used to wipe her pussy with every morning, and smeared amniotic fluid, blood and mucus out of the baby's eyes and nose. When she was done she cut the umbilical cord with a pair of hair scissors.

And They Call Me God

"He's perfect, Cindy. Oh, my God can you believe it? You actually had a fucking baby in this bitch!" She wrapped the infant in the towel and handed him to her, stealing additional gazes as Cindy pressed him against her bosom.

Taking in the moment, Cindy looked down at him, smiling widely. "I can't believe I did this!" She looked at her sister. "I can't believe God trusted me with something like this. He must be just as crazy as my ass!"

"I don't know why you so shocked," Angela said as she stood up, walked to the dresser and grabbed a pack of cigarettes. She tapped the carton, slid one out and lit it. "You a better mother than the ones I see running around this bitch. Plus you got me! We gonna be all right. Just gotta keep him quiet and out of folks way." She inhaled and blew out a puff of smoke and grew serious. "And keep *him* away from the baby, Cindy. Don't let him come around since he made a decision not to be in the kid's life."

Cindy looked down at the afterbirth sliding out of her. "Look at my body, Angela. Look at what he did to me. The last thing I feel like doing is seeing Eugene's face."

"I know you. You just like mama. So in love with dick you forget about the man it's attached to." She pointed at her with the cigarette. "Stay away from that nigga. We gonna get our lives together for the baby and we don't need him messing with our plans."

Cindy laughed. "Leave it alone, Angela."

"I'm serious!" she paused. "If he doesn't want to be a father he doesn't need no pussy either."

Cindy gazed at her and then the baby. "I'm calling him Devonte."

Angela sighed. "Please don't call him that evil shit."

"Well I'm his mother and it sounds like a heartbreaker name to me," she looked down at him and kissed him on the forehead. "Wait and see. Women will fall at his feet."

"This my nephew." Angela tapped the cigarette butt, plopping ashes to the floor as if it were a huge ashtray. "If I don't do nothing else I'll see him be the man I know he can. With or without you."

✝
5 YEARS LATER

Angela stood in the grimy kitchen, her long legs hung out of the white waitress uniform she donned, as she prepared her nephew's dinner. The familiar scent of the cocoa butter lotion she always wore made her smell sweet as ever. With less than an hour to be at work she had to prepare something quick and she knew just the meal...black folk's spaghetti— Oodles of Noodles.

Of course Cindy claimed she couldn't cook for her own son because she was sick but Angela knew she was just salty. Earlier in the day Cindy asked if Angela could watch Devonte and she said no. Unlike other nights, this time she would be forced to watch her own child.

Besides, if Angela missed the bus again she might have to walk ten miles or jack a stranger's dick for a ride. It was either those scenarios or risk getting fired which was not an option. No matter how hard she had to go Angela had a plan and she was sticking to it. She was saving enough money to finally get them out of Myers and into a place of their own, where Devonte didn't need to be hidden like a bad secret.

When the Oodles of Noodles were ready, she poured them in a yellow bowl, chopped up some boiled eggs and added a little soy sauce just the way her nephew liked.

When she gazed down at him he was staring up at her, wide eyed and hungry. She smiled and rubbed his little head roughly. "What you looking at, little man?"

"My food," he pointed.

She frowned. "What you talking about? This for me," she said with a serious face. "You not getting none of this."

"You wanna fight?" he asked playfully, putting his fists up in the air.

She pretended to be scared. "Naw, you got it, Devonte. I'm too afraid to go to blows with you." She winked at him. "Now go on back in the room before somebody catches you out here and snitches."

He rushed down the hall and into the room.

She was almost done when Matthew Steadman walked up to her with the stank of evil. An army veteran, he was a tall, lanky, middle-aged man with goggle eyes. A dark presence always followed him and meshed into the soul of anyone he approached. "Where you going, sexy?" he ran his tongue over his lips that were so dry she could hear them scratching against his tongue.

Disgusted she rolled her eyes. "After I eat I'm going to work."

"You know I got money right." He gripped his penis. "Plenty…and all you have to do is submit. When you gonna realize you making life harder on yourself?"

She picked up the bowl and looked into his eerie face. "First off you live here with me so how you got more money? Second of all I'm never fucking you or submitting. So get over it or kill yourself trying."

His expression flattened and his eyes narrowed. "Is it true ya'll have a kid living here?" he asked in a conniving tone. "That's right…I heard you got some boy child staying here when you know the rules."

She wanted to kill his ass for even mentioning her nephew. "We're adults now, Matthew. Even if we had a kid in our room so what?" she asked knowing it

And They Call Me God

didn't make any difference if they were over twenty-one.

"Adults or not, nobody supposed to be in the house unless it's run past the program directors. You and your sister practically living here for free and at the very least you're supposed to pay extra for him. I don't care if the little nigga's balls dropped or not."

Angela could feel her heart rate increase due to his threat although she tried to hide it. The last thing she needed was to be kicked out, forced to find a place to stay before they were ready.

"We ain't got no kid, Matthew. And if you keep making shit up you're bound to have an accident."

"You threatening me?"

Angela stepped back and leaned on the counter. "Did you ever wonder what happened to Louis from down the hall? He made similar accusations and found himself in the hospital for a week with a broken neck. After that nobody has seen him since." Although she had nothing to do with his absence, rumors on his whereabouts were whispered around the home like famous ghost stories so she used it toward her advantage.

In fear, Matthew backed up and looked her over.

"Stay out my way," she said as she grabbed the bowl, walked around him and toward her room.

Eager to tell Cindy how she punked Mathew again, she was thrown off when she opened the door and saw Devonte sitting on the bed *alone*, eating chocolate chip cookies.

The open window behind him indicated that Cindy didn't give a fuck that she had to go to work or not. Because she bounced anyway.

So selfish!

So rude!

Angela's temples pulsed with hate.

By T. Styles   23

She scrunched her face up in anger and then released the tension, when she saw Devonte staring at her. Closing the door behind herself, she locked it and walked over to him. The cool air from the open window tickled her face before she slammed it down with her free hand. "Hungry?"

He nodded and she couldn't help but fall deeper in love. His innocent eyes, open face and adorable smile stole all of the irritability she felt for Cindy. For the time being anyway.

"Did your mother say where she was going?" she took a seat on the edge of the bed, pulled the table toward them and placed the bowl on top of it. There was a fork on the table that she wiped on her uniform before putting it in the bowl.

He shook his head no.

She sighed heavily and her jaws clinched. "Devonte, I want to ask you something and I want you to tell me the truth."

"Okay," he said sweetly.

"When I'm gone to work, does your mother leave you here by yourself?"

He nodded yes and picked up the fork.

Her throat felt like it was closing up and a wave of pain rolled across her forehead. She needed him to step up and watch himself but she was afraid. Although she loved her nephew, he had a problem with whining. He whined for attention. He whined for hugs and he whined if he felt it would get him what he wanted. The last thing she needed was him whining when she wasn't in the house.

"Would you be scared if I left for work and came back later? I'll bring you some McDonalds."

He dipped the fork into the bowl. "Can I go to Wanda's?"

She frowned because she wondered how he knew anybody else but them. "Wanda?"

"When mama leaves, Wanda opens the door and comes into the room sometimes. She gives me kisses and candy. She's nice."

Comes into the room? She thought.

Angela didn't want to scare her nephew but she needed to know what the drug addict from down the hall was doing in her personal space. "What does she do in here?"

"Looks for stuff," he shrugged filling his mouth. Noodles hung out the corners of his lips. "You want me to tell her not to come in next time?"

No longer hearing her nephew, Angela popped up and moved toward the door. "I'll be right back. Don't move."

Angela approached Wanda's door with clenched fists readying to pound on that bitch. Once there she banged so hard her knuckles bled and leaked into the wood. When Wanda opened it, her hair was matted to her head and her clothing soiled with yesterday's meal, Angela started to say never mind. The last thing she wanted to do was touch anything on her nasty body and that included her face.

Amazingly, although she was disheveled, she was still an attractive woman.

Wanda was a veteran who joined the army over ten years ago to deal with the emotions she had from a troubled life. She figured if she carried a gun in the service, no one would try to hurt her anymore and her problems would vanish.

She was mistaken.

After becoming disabled due to a grenade explosion and shrapnel entering her scalp, she was honorably discharged and given disability income. Although most of the money she received was spent within the hour she cashed it due to her love affair with heroin.

"What the fuck was you doing in my room?" Angela asked harshly.

Wanda was about to close the door in her face but Angela pushed it backwards and entered without invitation. Surprisingly her room was neat and clean and Angela wondered why her person was so grimy.

"My nephew told me you been in my space, bitch." She looked around. "What were you doing?"

In defense mode she said, "That little ass nigga is not supposed to even be in this—"

Wanda's words were trapped in her throat when Angela hit her in the gut so hard she expelled a puff of air that smelled like old bologna. When Wanda fell on the bed Angela looked down at her. "I'ma ask you again what were you doing in my room?"

Afraid, Wanda sat up straight, rubbed her belly and exhaled. "I was looking for something to sell."

"You mean to steal." She responded.

Stomach still throbbing she asked, "Does it matter?"

"How you even know he was in my spot by himself?"

"Girl everybody knows that shit. When your sister has him she forgets to feed him, so I do. You should be thanking me instead of assaulting me."

Angela's eyes rolled upward as her sister's shiftlessness came into her mind. "So she leaves him with you?"

"Sometimes...but never too long."

Angela couldn't get over how ignorant and irresponsible Cindy was. Who could care less? Devonte wasn't supposed to be anywhere near other houseguests. "Look, I need you to do me a favor." She stepped closer.

Suspiciously, "Why should I do anything for you?"

"Because you could make some money and it will prevent me from kicking your ass for being in my room when I'm not home." She paused. "Ass kicking now or the favor. Your call."

Wanda wiped her hand down her face and realized she needed to relent. "Okay, but let me clear a few things up." She made probing eye contact. "I watch kids how I watch kids. I don't want nobody telling me how to take care of him, or what to do while he's in my room. If you can't get with that you can just beat my ass because for real I don't care."

Something told her not to leave her nephew with the woman but she was in a bind. "Okay. Whatever...as long as he's safe."

"He will be." Projecting a louder voice she said, "But you better talk to him about crying too. Because the moment he whines his little ass is out of here."

Angela packed Devonte's book bag and before she walked him to Wanda's she looked down at him. It was time to get him straight before going any further. The last thing she needed was Devonte being brought back to the room by Wanda because of his crying. But what could she say that would pack a hard enough punch?

He was a child.

After scanning her mind on what to say that would be the most effective she picked up the Bible her social worker gave her years ago. She would scare him into submission. "You know what this is?" she asked gripping the book so hard it dented under her fingertips.

He shook his head no.

She bent down so that they were eye to eye. "It's a Bible," she whispered as if telling a ghost story. "And it has a lot about little boys who cry too much or disobey parents and adults. So you gotta be good, Devonte. Because if you don't God will be mad at you."

"What...what will he do to me?" he stuttered.

Angela examined him and having zero knowledge about the Word she decided to lie. "If you disobey the Bible the penalty is death." She saw he was scared and went harder. "Do you want to die?"

He shook his head no.

"Then act like your little ass got some sense, or else."

✝

Wanda sat on the bed with Devonte watching TV, with her blue velvet robe hanging open showcasing her limp breasts. Her intentions were to seduce but he was too young so he wasn't receptive. Unable to hold back she asked, "You wanna kiss me, Devonte?" she pointed at her mouth. "Right here?"

He shook his head no.

She eyed him furtively. "Well I don't care what you want. Come do it anyway," she frowned.

He got up, walked in front of her and kissed her on the lips. Disgusted at how she smelled and how creepy she was behaving, he felt himself about to cry. Sensing this, she roughly grabbed him by the shoulders and stared down at him. "You want me to tell your aunt you acting like a sissy? So she'll get rid of you?"

He shook his head no.

Believing he would not do the things she wanted she decided to go harder. "I see you got that Bible over there. Did you know that Jesus sacrificed himself for us? Do you know what that means?"

"No." His bottom lip popped in and out of his mouth in an attempt not to cry.

"It means he gave himself over to the people...like you have to give yourself over to me." She paused. "If you do you'll be a God like Jesus. Don't you wanna be a God?"

He nodded yes, not fully knowing what she meant.

"Then come over here and prove it, before I get angry."

Angela and Devonte were asleep when the window above their heads opened, bringing with it a gush of cool air that tickled their faces. Cindy slid inside, legs first, doing her best not to wake up anyone.

She was filled with Eugene's semen and eager to wash out her pussy and go to sleep.

While she was on creep mode, Angela eased out of bed, walked up to the window, crossed her arms over her chest and waited. When Cindy was fully inside and turned around, Angela slapped her so hard in the face her legs buckled.

By T. Styles 29

Her hair was in scattered mess. "What the fuck is wrong with you?" Cindy yelled touching the place she'd been struck...her cheek and lips burned like fire.

"Do you love him?" Angela asked.

"Of course I do! That's why I left today even though you said you wouldn't watch Devonte!"

"I ain't talking about that nigga out there on the street! I'm talking about your son, bitch!" Angela responded through clenched teeth.

"Don't ask me no shit like that. You know how I feel about my child." She walked around her and sat on the edge of the bed. "I think Devonte being with you so much is making you think he's yours."

"Answer the question!"

She placed a pad of hair behind her ear but it was so stiff it popped back out. "Yes I love my son, bitch!"

"Then why are you deliberately fucking up his head?" she paused. "Don't you realize that his mother not being in his life is setting him up for failure? He already don't have a father!"

"And you telling me this while he's in the room is helping him how?"

Angela moved closer, bent down and got in her face. "You are worthless! You were right, God had no business making you his mother."

Cindy stood up calmly and got in her face. When she was ready she brought her forearm over Angela's head causing her to plummet to the floor. In beat mode, Cindy pounced on Angela and started striking her. They bit and clawed into each other's skin as if they were unrelated.

Each trying to overpower the other.

All the while Devonte sat on the bed, Bible pressed against his face in an attempt to smother his cries.

And They Call Me God

Angela and Cindy sat on the edge of the bed with Devonte looking at the movie *The Wiz*—their faces scarred and punctured like they were in a heavyweight bout. Although the sisters were momentary enemies four days ago, they put the melee behind them to focus on family.

Ironically things were going smoothly. Cindy hadn't seen Devonte's father in days and Angela got someone to cover her shift at work for a week to spend more time home. Although she claimed to want to repair her family, in actuality she didn't trust Cindy with her own self or her nephew. So they lived off the money Angela saved for their new apartment, believing she would make it up later...after the Eugene crisis was over.

They were in the middle of the movie when there was a soft knock at the window. When they turned around, through the crooked blinds they could see Eugene's nostrils.

Angela looked toward Cindy waiting for her to do what was necessary...get rid of him. But it was clear from the wide-eyed grin on Cindy's face that she was happy to see him and incapable of turning him away on her own. "Let me go outside and talk to him for a moment," Cindy begged.

Angela turned the television volume down. "This time is supposed to be for Devonte." She paused. "Come on, Cindy. You promised." She looked over at Devonte who was silent although wanting the same—for his mother to stay.

Cindy gave a halfhearted shrug. "I guess I'll tell him to leave then," Cindy said as she gazed at Devonte and then the window. Every cell of her being wanted to bounce with Eugene but she didn't want to piss off her sister who didn't have a problem fighting to the death. Her jaw still hurt from the last battle and she simply wasn't in the mood.

"Thank you," Angela said.

Irritated with her sister and son, Cindy pushed open the window. "Hey, Eugene…" she sighed.

Eugene stuck his head into the window and with wild eyes staring inside, beyond his son he said, "That's all you have to say to me? I been locked up for a few days, baby. Sorry I didn't check you earlier but I thought you'd be happier to see me. You coming out?"

Cindy looked back at Devonte and then Eugene. With a deflated chest she said, "I'm gonna spend time with my son today."

He chuckled. "Spend time with your son? What the fuck?" he frowned. "You been in the house for days now, right?" He paused. "I figured you'd miss me by now. Where is my time?"

"I do…its just that I promised Angela and…" she paused and grew excited when another idea entered her mind. "You want to come inside and hang out with me and Devonte?" she asked, hoping he'd say the right thing.

His face held an unkind smile. "Uh…yeah, I can hang out with the kid for a minute and then we can go to the club. My man is on the door tonight and he'll let us in for free." He looked over at Devonte as if he were a stinky nuisance. "You want your pops to hang out with—"

Not going for the foolishness Angela unleashed on him. "Get the fuck up out my window, Eugene," she said wasting no time on the games.

"What you talking about, let me see my kid!"

Angela stood up and approached him. "Devonte is not hanging with you and neither is Cindy. Now get the fuck from in front the window before you lose a set of teeth." She picked up the baseball bat that always rested near the bed...for unexpected intruders.

Eugene forced away a frown. "If that's how you want it." He looked at Cindy and then back at Angela. "Word to the wise, make that the last time you threaten me." He stormed away with ideas of the things he would do to her if he ever got her alone.

But instead of letting Cindy go, he returned, every night for weeks. When Angela had to go to work she paid Wanda to room-sit, making sure to hide all of her valuables first. This way she could ensure Devonte wasn't alone and Cindy didn't leave.

Trying to control things, Angela was hoping that Eugene would move on but he didn't. Cindy was the only person alive who thought Eugene was smart. She would laugh at his jokes, cling to him like a dryer sheet and tell him how she would die if she couldn't be with him.

Since he was a miserable drunk with delusions of grandeur he needed her to feel better about himself. So Eugene's plan was simple, fake a desire to be with his son by convincing Angela that he changed. Because the only person who controlled Cindy more than him was Angela.

During the third week Eugene returned and Angela, having had two glasses of wine earlier in the evening, showed mercy and allowed him inside. Playing smart, instead of approaching Cindy who was so excited to see him she couldn't contain herself, he bypassed her with a new pair of Nike Air Jordon's. He made his son the apple of his eyes.

The shoes were the only things he'd ever bought for the kid.

By T. Styles   33

First Eugene showed him how to tie up his new sneaks and then he showed him how to keep them clean. When he was done they talked about everything from girls to how to fight and Angela liked having him around. It was then that Angela could see why Cindy worshiped him so much. He possessed charisma and spoke in a low hypnotic tone. Eugene showed up everyday for one week straight and Angela got so comfortable that she stopped having Wanda come over.

Things were looking good until three weeks later when Angela came home late after a long day of waitressing. She stepped into her room and was surprised that her nephew or Cindy were home. Since she knew she'd left him with Cindy she grew worried, thinking that Devonte may have been out on the streets because she wasn't watching him. Her sister's antics were bringing stress on her body and she found herself resenting her for it. She was about to lose it until something in her mind whispered...*Wanda's.*

On the hunt, Angela rushed out of the room and down the hall to her room. She knocked a few times but when she saw the door was open, she pushed her way inside. "Wanda," she yelled.

No one was in the bedroom, she thought until suddenly, Wanda, dressed in a house robe, hurried out of the small bathroom within her room.

Angela said, "Do you know where..."

When she saw Devonte following Wanda out of the bathroom she was confused. Fixing her stares on Wanda and then Devonte she knew something was off. "Oh...he's here," Angela said.

"I'm sorry. I forgot to leave you a note, girl," Wanda smiled snatching her robe tighter. She looked at

And They Call Me God

Devonte and then back at Angela. "What you doing here so early?"

"Where is Cindy?" she asked in a flat tone.

"She went with Eugene somewhere. They paid me a few bucks to watch him. Why?" she frowned. "Is everything okay?"

"What were you doing in the...bathroom?"

"Nothing. Just taking a bath." She looked at Devonte. "And he had to pee so he went in too."

There wasn't any steam flowing out of the bathroom and Wanda damn sure didn't smell like soap. Angela sensed foul play and thought about pursuing the matter but the truth was she didn't want to know. She elected to remain ignorant to an idea that scared her so much it was paralyzing...that her beloved nephew was being sexually abused.

Not only that, deep inside she knew that without Wanda's help that she couldn't keep her job because her sister was simply unreliable. The worst-case scenario, as far as Angela was concerned, was that he would endure whatever he was going through, and then when she saved up more money, she would move them out. Besides, in her opinion he was a little boy and he probably liked it anyway.

At least she hoped.

Angela walked up to Devonte and grabbed is hand. "I'm so sick of your fucking mother," she said skipping the subject purposely to clear her mind. "Come on, boy. And wipe that dumb look off your face. I'm about to feed you," she continued as if hunger was the reason for his dismay.

On the way down the hall, Devonte gripped her hand tightly, preparing to tell her about the things he experienced under Wanda's watch. "Auntie...I..."

"Shut up, boy," she said cutting him off. "Just shut up before somebody hears you talking all loud." She pulled his arm and rushed him down the hallway. "You not even supposed to be living in the house!"

If anybody was loud it was Angela. Guilt weighed down on her and caused her to act irrationally. But she needed her thoughts on anything except the truth, while she silently prayed that when he was older he wouldn't hate her for that exact moment...the day he tried to express himself in a dirty hallway and was silenced.

She pulled him all the way to their room and slammed the door, waking every neighbor along the way in the process.

✝

TEN YEARS LATER

Angela's plans for a better life didn't pan out...

Although they weren't living in the room, they remained in the same house. The only thing changed was that Angela, Cindy and Devonte now rented the lower half of the home. The two-bedroom unit wasn't large enough for a fifteen-year-old kid and two thirty-something year old adults, but at least they didn't have to hide Devonte any longer.

Since they paid two hundred dollars more, it meant they made their own rules and got a little more space. Besides, the Myers home had lost its credentials as a government funded agency long ago due to the poor condition of the house. All children and dependent veterans were removed, leaving behind the scavengers who were too pitiful to move on.

Cindy wept on a broken down picnic table in the backyard just as fifteen-year-old Devonte walked outside. Worried over her mental condition, which seemed to be deteriorating daily, he rushed toward her. "Ma, why you crying?" he asked rubbing her back. "You hurt?"

"Get the fuck off me," she yelled with a flailing arm that almost slapped him in the face. "I want Eugene! All I ever wanted was Eugene and it's your fault he isn't around anymore!"

"Ma, he coming back," Devonte said softly, trying desperately to console a woman who couldn't give a fuck about him. "Come in the house...I'll make you one of the drinks you like."

She rocked back and forth like a fiend. "I don't want anything! All I want to know is where's Eugene!?"

"Maybe he's locked up again."

"You don't know him," she spit. "You don't know anything about your father! He's a good man! He been trying to get himself together and everything."

Hearing the commotion Angela walked outside to check on the matter. Years of Cindy's unstable behavior had taken its toll on her face, arresting her beauty in the process. "Cindy, please come inside before our nosey ass neighbors think they know our business again." She looked around at a few backyards, noticing that already Cindy gained an audience.

Irritated with her presence, she stood up and glared at Angela. Her foot pressed against one of the many empty beer cans on the ground as she struggled to balance herself. "I'm so fucking sick of your shit, Angela! Sick of you trying to get me to be someone I ain't. Sick of pretending I know how to be a mother. And sick of living in this hellhole!" Cindy stormed away.

"Come on in the house, Devonte," Angela said softly. Her heart broke a little more every time she saw the pain broadcast on his face, courtesy of a mother who didn't know he was alive. "She'll be back soon." Angela looked into the direction she ran, over the bent fence and into the city. "Where else will she go?"

When Devonte walked into the room from school, he saw Angela pacing and biting on her bottom lip so hard it bled. Trying to do something with her hands, she squirted some cocoa butter lotion in her palm and rubbed back and forth, nervously.

Something was off and he felt it. Originally he was hungry but now food seemed to be the least of his troubles. He placed his pencil on the table and his book back on the chair and remained in place. Crossing his arms over his stomach he dropped them and prepared for what he assumed would be the worst. "What's wrong?"

Her shoulders curved forward. "It's your mother."

Devonte's stomach whirled. "What about her?"

"Somebody found her driver's license at a rest stop in Pennsylvania." A cold energy seemed to steal the space between them. "They think something happened to her."

Devonte looked at his aunt with wide eyes. He trudged toward the bed and plopped down. "Do they think she...they think she may be..."

"Don't say that dumb shit, Devonte." She rocked slightly. "I don't know where she is and you don't either," she continued knowing what he thought

And They Call Me God

because she considered the same fate. "Look, go down Wanda's for the night." She grabbed her purse and the bat against the wall. "I'm going out to look for her."

His temples throbbed. "Aunt Angela, do I have to? I'm fifteen and can watch myself."

"Yes you do," she said as she grabbed her purse. "Besides, she just got her food stamps and we don't have anything to eat here. The last thing I need is to be worrying about you not eating. Go to her house unless you want to starve," she walked around him and out the door.

Devonte sucked Wanda's breast the way she liked as she palmed the back of his head. She tasted like ashes in his mouth and he wanted her to finish doing whatever she needed to be satisfied, so that he could be left alone to watch TV. Luckily for him her pleasure was halted with a firm knock at the door.

Afraid she would be caught; Wanda closed her robe and shot Devonte and evil glare. She was reminding him to fix his expression, which screamed, *I hate you bitch.*

When his mien was replaced with indifference, Wanda stood up and opened the door. "Hey, girl," she said guiltily. "You back early. I didn't get a chance to feed Devonte yet."

Angela dragged her palms down her pants as if she was trying to get something off her hands. "Devonte, go to our apartment," she said lifelessly.

He stood up and approached. "You okay, Auntie?"

She avoided eye contact. "Just go to the apartment."

He quickly obeyed leaving them alone.

Distraught, Angela walked inside and sat on the edge of Wanda's bed as she closed and locked the door. "Do you hurt him when you're together?" Angela's eyes remained on the floor as she awaited the answer to her question.

"W...what you talking about?" Wanda stuttered sitting in an old wooden chair across from her.

Angela raised her eyes, and looked in her direction. "I asked...do you hurt him when you're together?"

Wanda swallowed; realizing Angela had her mind made up about what she thought was going on. "No...I don't. He happens to like me and I like him. I know he's young but back in the 1800's young men and older women got together all the time."

Angela laughed although she was repulsed at Wanda, and herself. "So you're doing him a favor huh?" she asked sarcastically as a frown appeared on her face.

"Why are you here?" Wanda said through pinched lips.

Silence.

Angela looked at her as if she were a piece of shit that grew wings and flew out of the toilet. "You are gross," she said.

"What are you talking about?" she paused. "You knew all along about me and Devonte. If you're coming at me now...if you're saying anything at all it means..."

Angela felt a hard cry coming but she suppressed it and exhaled instead. "She's dead," she said, her words were like faint lines of fog, almost unnoticeable. "My fuckin' sister is dead and I don't know how to tell my nephew," she said louder. "They didn't even have a relationship and now they never will!" she looked at

And They Call Me God

Wanda hoping she could provide comfort. "What am I going to do? I don't know how to be without Cindy. Since we were kids my world revolved around her. What now?"

"I'm so sorry, Angela," she said, not having another response available. The truth was she wanted her to leave so that she could get high. Sad stories always reminded her of the days she was electrocuted by her cousins for their pleasure before they beat and raped her.

"You got something in here?" Tears rolled slowly down her cheek.

Wanda frowned. "Got something...like what?"

"Whatever you use to make the pain go away."

Wanda shook her head back and forth. "No, I can't...I can't do that to you, Angela. Once you're on that shit there's no coming back from it."

Angela dug into her pocket and pulled out twenty-five bucks, before slapping it on the table. "Whatever it is, hook me up."

Wanda looked at the money, already salivating about what drugs she'd buy later. Besides, it wasn't like she'd have to give her the whole bump. Just a little prick would have the new blood on cloud nine, leaving the rest for herself.

Slowly Wanda walked toward her dresser and pulled out her kit— a bent spoon, needle, syringe, rubber tubing, tin foil, a lighter, cotton and a glassine envelope filled with heroin. She spread it out on the table next to her and when the shot was ready she looked over at Angela, "Are you sure about this?"

Angela stood up, raised her long sleeve shirt and sat down in another chair next to Wanda. She pointed at her blue vein and said, "Do it."

With the needle hovering over her flesh she said, "I will never accept the guilt for this shit."

By T. Styles 41

"Cheer up," she said sarcastically. "You stole my nephew's soul, now you can have mine."

MONTHS LATER

Ever since Cindy died and Angela got caught up on drugs Devonte's life grew harder. He stayed in the home, alone most of the time and saw things no child should have to.

After the first few months, strangely enough, he grew to enjoy Wanda's company and even felt he loved her. If he wasn't running errands, he took to robbing unsuspecting pedestrians so that Wanda could have enough money for her habit. He became her personal goon and she exploited him to the fullest. But Devonte didn't mind because she looked for him when he wasn't home. She fed him when Angela had given up the responsibility and she told him everyday how powerful he was.

"You are so smart, Devonte," she would tell him repeatedly. "But you have to watch them other women. They're scandalous. You can only trust me because I care about you. Remember that."

To a young man with nothing, Wanda's constant brainwashing disguised as love was everything.

With the drug addiction taking more real estate over Angela's life, after awhile she spent so much time in the streets that she often forgot where she lived. It was Devonte who went looking for her, only to help put her back on her feet. That included feeding her, cleaning her blood-crusted heroin tracks, funky hair and even horrendous smelling vagina.

He loved his aunt and held on to the hope that one day, with a lot of love she would return to him as strong as he remembered. At the age of fifteen, he found himself the caregiver of two emotionally damaged women and ironically he felt needed.

He would be their savior.

Throughout the months things changed with him. He grew clumsy at times, tripping and bumping into things, which irritated Wanda to no end. She knew during those times his mind was elsewhere, on his aunt, and she started to look forward to the days that Angela would hit the streets again so she could have him to herself.

But Devonte didn't care how Wanda felt about Angela. He was growing older and more rebellious and as a result he was starting to make his own decisions. And one of them was that he would always look after Angela, and if Wanda didn't like it she could kill herself with or without assistance.

One day he came home from his last day of school due to his decision to quit, only to be greeted by his grandmother—Aubrey Jenkins, whom he never met. She was a tall frail looking woman, with bluish grey hair. The frown lines surrounding the orifices of her face told she'd been through hell and possessed many stories to tell.

"Who you?" Devonte asked not afraid but not happy to see her either.

"I'm your father's mother," she said softly. "The name's Aubrey."

He laughed. "I ain't got no father."

She smiled. "I can see how you would think that. He ain't been much of a parent so I don't expect you to give him the credit or the glory. Hell, he and I don't even have a relationship."

He laughed. "So you abandoned your son too."

She frowned. "It's always easier speaking about things you know nothing of," she said softly. "Anyway, your aunt Angela called and asked me to come. So here I am."

Now she had his full attention. "Come here for what?" he frowned. "Is my aunt okay?" After being dealt the blow of losing his mother he wasn't in a position to lose his aunt too.

"She enrolled herself into a rehab program in California, Devonte. She wanted to say goodbye but the people said she had to leave at that moment, or risk losing her spot altogether. Since it's a grant program for first time users, she jumped at the opportunity. And considering the condition of her life I don't blame her."

She looked around the raggedy home while Devonte's heart felt like it sank in his chest upon hearing the news but he didn't want her to know.

He walked over to the kitchen table, bumping into the chair, before picking up a pack of cigarettes. He also placed on a pair of oversized shades to conceal the pain in his eyes.

"You walk just like your father," she declared. "You sound like him too." She paused. "I was even surprised that your mother gave you his last name...Harrington."

"Whenever I think about the father you talk so highly about, I also think about my mother's death."

"He didn't have anything to do with that," she said defensively.

"I know," he paused. "He was probably locked up as usual. But my mother went looking for him and a killer got to her and sliced her throat before throwing her body on the side of the highway like trash. So he is still responsible. Without him my mother would still be alive."

"But there would be no you."

"I would trade places with my mother in a heart beat." He paused. "Now that we've gotten that out of the way, I still don't know what you want."

Aubrey cleared her throat because she hadn't expected him to be so deep. "Your father has moved to another state. He needed to get away from it all and that included your mother."

He laughed. "Coward."

Devonte was shooting daggers and she felt anger brewing inside of her. Until she realized his feelings were warranted. A boy without a father was anger's son. "Your aunt wants you in a safer place then this and she's selected one...Dove's School For Boys." She paused. "It's a home for children in Baltimore who are displaced or without a parent."

"I'm not going to no home for niggas," he said. "I'm not supposed to be there no how. I'm not displaced. I live right here.

"But you won't make it by yourself."

"I'm a God, and Gods always survive." He smoked his cigarette and Aubrey walked closer.

"Son, do you want to see your aunt again? Do you want her to get well so you two can be together again?" she looked around. "Because that's the plan. That's why she wants you away from here, and away from that woman down the hall. She can't focus on her sobriety if she's worrying about you."

"You know about her? Wanda?"

"Yes, I know about that pedophile."

"It's easier speaking about things you know nothing of," he said stealing her words.

"Touche," she responded under her breath. "Devonte, I know you don't like me but I'm here for you. If you want to come with me and fulfill your aunt's dream then you have to leave now because I'm not coming back. Put your feelings aside." She looked at him.

He examined her appearance. "You look well off. How come I can't stay with you?"

"I appreciate the compliment but don't let the clothes fool you. I've collected some fine things over the course of my lifetime. But when it comes to a place to live I come up short. I simply don't have enough space. If I did I would, Devonte."

"I feel like a burden," he admitted.

"You're never a burden when there is at least one person who loves you."

DOVE'S HOME FOR BOYS
Baltimore, Maryland

Dove's Home For Boys, nestled in the middle of a halo of trees, housed fifty dislocated youths. Due to limited contact, the lateritious colored residence appeared separated from the rest of the state. And during darker days, in which the vilest acts occurred, the boys impacted felt as if they were separate from the rest of the planet.

Divorced from his aunt Angela and Wanda, Devonte lie quietly on the bottom bunk in a dorm style room, while his roommates, Stanford, Harper and Wayne, three knuckleheads who were also cousins, plotted their next venture.

Throughout the weeks, Devonte heard from no one and silently prayed that they hadn't forgotten about him. That he wouldn't be swept away, like white lint on a dark carpet.

He was invisible and had the need of companionship so great, that it crippled his movements within the house, forcing him into a place of internal seclusion that felt like hell. Although Devonte did all he could to show the boys that he could be as devious as them if given a chance, they never listened.

How could he convince them? He contemplated savagery...but who would suffer from his quest to belong?

"I'm telling you we can do this," Stanford said as he stood in front of the other two in the middle of the room. The gap between his teeth caused each word uttered to be introduced by a soft whistle. "All we gotta do is wait until they get together and grab 'em. It ain't like they don't do the same thing every Friday."

"You talking crazy," Harper said with wide eyes. His skin was as chocolate as his cousins, but his thinner grain of hair made him appear to be mixed with something other than African American—but he wasn't. "I don't got a good feeling 'bout this. The last time we got in trouble they put us in the Solitude Room for a month. If they catch us again we'll be up shit's creek."

"Fuck is a shit's creek?" Wayne asked as he scratched his wooly hair. He was growing agitated because the longer they procrastinated to grab the keys to Mr. Tower's car, the harder it would be to get out of the house and make it to their older cousin's party in the county. "All I want to know is are we moving out or not?"

The three cousins looked at one another with Devonte as their only audience member.

"Let's go then," Stanford said unsure of himself.

When nobody moved for the door it became obvious…all three were scared and all three were going nowhere. The risk was too great and nobody was willing to take it. Hampered, they walked toward their beds to prepare for sleep.

Stanford, Harper and Wayne resigned to sleeping when a pair of keys jingled quietly in the dark room. Upon hearing clinking, Stanford was the first to open his eyes, as he flipped on the lamp to be able to see who was making the soft noise. To his surprise he saw Devonte, standing with the keys in his palm. "Is this what you were looking for?"

Excitedly, Stanford hopped out of bed and looked at the keys as if they were the Holy Grail. Stanford didn't know if he was more enthusiastic about being able to go to the party, or Devonte's diligence. It didn't matter at the moment…because of Devonte the night was not lost.

Stanford grabbed the keys from his hands and looked back at his cousins. "We going after all." He looked at Devonte. "Thanks to our new friend."

Wayne and Harper popped out of bed and wondered if they were dreaming. When they saw the leather and gold Honda key chain they knew it was real. So they quickly got dressed, eased out of the window and jumped in the car with Stanford driving.

After the key heist, which was easy for Devonte, he became a regular member of the trio turned quartet. The car seize, the first of many, happened as a result of Mr. Towers being so consumed with the softness of Mrs. Locket's pussy, who he had bent over the edge of his desk, that there could've been a war outside and he would've been none the wiser. His pants lay in front of his office's door, in a hump, and Devonte slipped the keys out without his knowledge.

Since Mr. Towers and Mrs. Locket were both exhausted after their rendezvous, they drifted off to sleep in the study, unaware that the boys even left the premises or returned the keys in the middle of the night when the party was over.

Throughout the weeks, suddenly, Devonte's life didn't seem so hard. He felt like a part of something…he felt like he had a family. Although they were a handful without him, with him they were sinister.

Devonte was always willing to do the things the others weren't. If they wanted money stolen from the resident managers, he was able to lift it. If they wanted extra snacks to sneak into their room, he was able to get them from the kitchen. Devonte was instrumental for the group and they all liked him except…Harper.

One raining day, Stanford, Harper and Wayne were in the recreation room playing pool when Harper decided to get a few things off his chest. He would've done it earlier but Devonte had become so instrumental that he went everywhere they went, leaving him with no chance for privacy. Since he shared their room Harper didn't have a break from him there either. But with Devonte in the nurse's office at the moment he decided to use this time to express his feelings.

"How do you feel about Devonte?" he asked as he stood behind Stanford who was holding the pool cue.

Stanford shot the white and yellow balls toward the corner pocket and missed, before handing the stick to Wayne. "What you mean?" he asked irritated he didn't hit his mark.

"I mean do you trust him?" he looked at both of them, before looking at the door for Devonte. He wanted to make sure Devonte wasn't coming back before he got things off his chest.

"He's a little clumsy but he's a stand up nigga," Wayne said as he shot for the corner pocket and succeeded. "If he was any less we wouldn't have him around us. Why you askin'?"

Harper moved around uneasily next to the table. He wiped his sweaty hands on his pants. "Well I don't trust him. I think it's just a matter of time before he snitches or gets us caught during a caper."

Stanford and Wayne laughed.

"Nigga, what the fuck is a caper first of all?" Stanford asked. "And secondly how would he catch us on it?"

They both chuckled harder, which angered Harper even more.

"Harp, I know you don't like new people but the kid been on point. It's because of him our lives in this bitch been easier. Don't fuck it up because you jealous."

His chin dipped downward. "Who said I was jealous?" he frowned. "I'm just saying we should be more careful about new niggas."

"You acting like you jealous to me," Wayne said.

Silence.

And They Call Me God

"It's like this, either get rid of him or I'm out. Blood or not." He stormed away, causing everyone in the recreation room to give him their undivided attention.

A few days later Stanford, Harper and Wayne were on their way to another party and although no one told Devonte about it, he got dressed knowing he was invited.

After the fake body pillows, that were meant to trick the resident managers who checked on the boys at night, were set up on their beds, they were ready to leave out of the bedroom window.

And Devonte followed.

Harper turned around and said, "What you doing?" The pleasure he got out of shutting him down felt so good his body trembled.

Devonte smiled, thinking he was playing. "Stop fucking around, Harp. I'm going to the party with ya'll."

"Who the fuck said you were invited?" Harper continued in a wide stance.

Devonte crossed his arms over his stomach before allowing them to fall at his sides. "But what about the keys?" He laughed, trying to make light of an embarrassing situation. "You need the keys right? I can go get 'em." He looked behind him at Stanford and Wayne.

Suddenly Wayne pulled them out of his pocket. "Got 'em already, cuz."

Devonte looked at Stanford, hoping for a punch line. "Is everything...like is everything cool with us?"

"Yeah, man," Stanford said softly. "We just going at it alone tonight." He looked at his cousins. "Let's leave before the residents do a room check." He lifted the window and eased out.

Once outside he closed the window, gazed at Devonte and walked away.

Pissy drunk, Stanford was in the communal shower at Dove's, barely able to stand on his feet. He and his cousins drank too much at the party but unlike them, he vomited all over his clothing and couldn't go straight to bed before cleaning up.

He was just about to get out when Devonte stepped behind him, wrapped his forearm around his throat and squeezed.

The entire night, Devonte sat in his bed as humiliation kept him company. Why were people always abandoning him? What did he have to do to prove he was worthy of love and acceptance? His questioning started out honest but turned dark the later it got.

Although Harper should've been his *real* target, seeing as though he started the wheels in motion to cut Devonte off, it was Stanford who broke his heart the most. It was Stanford who ran the group and it was Stanford who could've fought for him.

So why didn't he?

It didn't matter.

It was too late.

When Stanford struggled to breathe within the death grip, Devonte pulled down his sweat pants with his other hand and gripped his penis as he sodomized him. Devonte didn't allow himself to entertain whether he was gay or not. It didn't matter.

When he was alone he searched his mind for the best way to break Stanford's spirit. Beating him up would be too easy but this…the effects were lasting.

And They Call Me God

Stanford did his best to struggle but he was no match for Devonte who was sober and angry. Succumbing to Devonte's torture, he fell on the floor face first, as Devonte continued to rape him until Stanford passed out from hurt and pain on the shower's floor.

When Devonte rose, the water washed away the semen and blood along with his anger.

MONTHS LATER

Devonte was slumped in the back of the cab and gazed out of the window at the blur of passing trees. He replayed the last few months of his life. After assaulting Stanford, Devonte was segregated to the Solitude Room for the rest of his stay...several months. Deemed dangerous, and rightfully so, the staff didn't feel comfortable releasing him amongst the other children.

It wasn't because Stanford communicated what happened to him. On the contrary, he never said a word and was eventually removed from Dove's and placed into a psychiatric hospital where he could get help.

It was one of the staff members, doing a night check, who saw the act. As a result, Devonte was sequestered until a new place could be found.

Although he should've been remanded to a facility for violent offenders, the home didn't want to risk more bad publicity so they swept it under the rug. Just get rid of the problem was the answer after a secret meeting amongst the staff members was held about the issue.

After a few months, when a new foster home was established, he was given his dismissal papers.

Lying on the bed, hands behind his head, face up, Devonte was making clicking noises with his mouth. He would start slow and then go faster. When there was a knock at the door he sat up to see who was coming inside.

"What was that noise?" Mr. Towers asked grumpily as he unlocked and opened the door.

"Nothing."

"Well get dressed," Mr. Towers said entering. "Your social worker will be here in an hour."

Devonte stood up, and grabbed his brown suitcase that sat next to the door. Mr. Towers' loud clacking shoes sounded off as Devonte followed. Several minutes later, Mr. Towers stopped at his office, which was located next to the front door.

They approached some chairs. "Sit right here," Mr. Towers said, giving Devonte a displeasing look. He crossed his arms over his chest. "I know you're leaving but it's disgusting how you treated that boy. He was a good kid who didn't deserve to be violated. I hope your actions keep you up at night."

Devonte blinked several times and grinned. "I wonder if Mrs. Locket gets wetter when you fuck her than she does with her husband."

Mortified, and wondering how Devonte knew about the affair, Mr. Towers hustled back into his office and slammed the door.

When he was gone, instead of waiting for his social worker Devonte slipped out of the facility, leaving his suitcase behind. As far as he was concerned the foster home could wait. He had other plans and nothing was going to stop him.

"You got my money?" the cab driver inquired after parking in front of a brick building.

Sighing, Devonte dug into his pocket and pulled out fifteen dollars. After the cab fare and an eighty-cent tip, he was officially broke. He paid the driver his fare and he stumbled out, knees pressing into the curb.

"You okay?" the driver asked.

Devonte stood up, brushed off his knees and slammed the door as his answer.

Carefully he wandered toward the building...the sound of his heartbeat thumped so loudly he could no longer hear the surroundings. He had gotten the address from a resident at the former Myers home and hoped it was correct. He spent all of the money he owned.

Originally he stopped by to see Wanda but learned that Matthew Steadman, the army vet who stayed there, while on a revenge mission murdered her. She wasn't even the real target.

The same night that Devonte was taken from Myers, by his grandmother, Matthew heard someone in Angela's room. Thinking it was Angela, oblivious to her being in rehab, he opened the door only to see Wanda snooping around. Afraid she would tell someone, he strangled her into silence, snuffing out her life. Someone heard the noise, saw him leaving and he was arrested for her murder.

Upon hearing the news Devonte was distressed but he realized he had to move on. Besides, he was use to heartache.

He was given an ounce of relief when someone within the home told him that he knew his aunt's whereabouts. Now it was time to be reunited.

Opening the building's door, he grabbed the rail and ascended up several steps before reaching apartment 7. When ready he took a deep breath and knocked on the door before stepping a few feet back. The moment he heard her voice his heart lit up.

"Just a minute," she said happily pulling the door open.

Devonte blinked a few times and smiled when he smelled the scent of his aunt's favorite cocoa butter lotion. He was overwhelmed with emotion to be in her presence but the surprised and disappointed look on her face made him think she didn't feel the same.

"Devon...Devonte," she stuttered. Her skin looked as if it had gone pale as she gazed upon him. "What are you doing here? I mean...how did you find me?"

Swallowing what was left of his pride he said, "You not happy to see me? Because I'm happy to see you."

With wild eyes rolling around him she said, "Of course...but I..."

"You look good, auntie," he said truthfully before looking down at himself. "I wish I could've looked nicer but I've been going through it. "

"Thank you for the compliment, Devonte. And I'm sorry to hear you've had trouble." She sighed. "I been clean for almost eight months now," she said proudly, gazing behind him at the door as if expecting someone else.

"You not going to invite me in?"

She held onto the doorknob, preventing his entrance as if he'd stolen from her before. "Devonte, I can't let you in and I can't let you stay here."

His jaw dropped and he crossed his arms over his stomach before releasing them at his sides, something he did whenever nervous or fearful. "But why...I...."

And They Call Me God

"You remind me of…"

"My mother," he said finishing her sentence.

"No. You remind me of losing her," she said softly. "I was able to get clean because I didn't have to see you, and be reminded that it was because of me that she's not here."

"But, aunt Angela, Aubrey said you wanted me to stay in that place until you got clean," he said as his palms moved forward. "You clean now. So please don't abandon me."

"Devonte, I'm not the same person you remember. I allowed a lot of pressure to be placed on myself by my sister and by taking care of you. I thought I had to take care of her after our parents died and when you were born I didn't get a chance to be a kid. I didn't get a chance to have a life…and I'm going to do that now."

"Without me…" he whispered.

"Hold on," she said entering her apartment, closing the door behind herself. She returned a minute later carrying a piece of paper, a Bible and fifty bucks. "This is your grandmother Aubrey's address. Go see her. I know this seems harsh but it's her and your father's turn to take care of you."

He frowned. "I would've expected this kinda shit from my mother…but never you."

"Devonte, you have to understand…"

"I let Wanda touch me…I even kissed her in ways I chose to forget," he said in a low vibrating voice. "I was a kid and I took it all because I didn't want you to worry about me. I didn't want you to have more pressure on yourself then you already did. I saw the pain in your eyes. But what about me? Don't I deserve relief?"

"Devonte, I didn't know —"

"You knew!" he yelled, his voice echoing throughout the hall before going silent. "Don't lie to me because I know you knew. I even tried to tell you in the hallway one day and you denied me that opportunity when I was five years old."

He grabbed the items she was holding. He stuffed the fifty bucks and the piece of paper in the Bible.

"You should know that I'm not the same person either," he continued. "You should also know that there is no need to worry about me. The darkness that you were afraid of getting to me outside on the streets lives in here," he said pointing at his chest. "And maybe it's best that you didn't let me in. I might be liable to take my hate out on you." He looked at her breasts, gripped his penis and walked away.

A FEW MONTHS LATER

Devonte sucked on Elizabeth Wu's pale breast so hard it was painful. At the same time he spread her legs and thrust into her hairy vagina with his penis using severe pressure.

She was not only his foster mother, but also the new love of his life. He needed her not only because his father, aunt and grandmother had abandoned him but also because she was the only person who claimed to need him.

Although most of her declarations were done in the bedroom, when her husband was not at home of course, he felt he contributed to her happiness in a special way. And for the moment that was all he needed.

And They Call Me God

Releasing her nipple from his lips he kissed her roughly, stuffing his tongue into the warmth of her mouth. "I love you, Elizabeth."

"I know honey," she said as she dug her fingernails into his lower back, directing his motions. "But don't stop moving that dick. Keep working it like I taught you. You're about to make me cum."

Devonte placed his face in the pit of her neck and inhaled her sweaty flesh, soaked with expensive Chanel Number 5 perfume. Unable to resist the sex appeal of a forty-three year old woman, he splashed his semen into her body as if she belonged to him.

He went limp in her arms.

"Don't stop, Devonte," she encouraged. "Just keep pumping me until you go soft. If I don't cum too I need you to lick it okay?"

He nodded, wanting eagerly to please her.

"What the fuck is going on?" Kyong Wu asked calmly.

Elizabeth pushed Devonte off of her body, fully prepared to cry rape, but it would be in vain. Kyong had been there for a minute and heard the coaching she'd given the boy before announcing himself. There was no use in her lying because he heard it all.

She huddled in the corner of the bed, the cum soaked sheets concealing her breasts and vagina. "Honey, I was just talking to—"

Kyong remained unperturbed as he walked past Devonte and made his way to his side of the bed. Elizabeth, sensing death in the air based on her husband's demeanor, picked up Devonte's jeans and pressed them against his chest. In fear for his life, her body trembling, she whispered, "Go. I'll meet you at the place we first met. Now!"

Devonte hurried down the stairs just before the first bullet slammed into the wall above his head. He didn't think it was possible but he was able to hop into his jeans and his shirt, all while running for his life. Youth and speed saved him as bullets, with his name on them, blasted through the air.

An hour later, shoeless and afraid, Devonte sat at a table in IHOP...he was waiting on his cherished Elizabeth. A cold plate of half eaten pancakes sat in front of him and before long night covered the small restaurant.

It was apparent a long time ago.

She wasn't coming.

Tears rolled down his face and his heart pounded in the partitions of his chest. He was use to feeling alone but once again he allowed himself to trust another.

Why was love never his?

Was he that deplorable?

Before he met the Wu's he lived on the streets for weeks...using robbery and stealing as his financiers. But when Child Protective Services discovered him drunk and dirty in a movie theater, he was placed in a foster home where Elizabeth took him under her wing and breasts.

Under expensive sheets speckled with her husband's dried semen, Elizabeth told Devonte about all the ways she would love him if he did what he was told. And when the sex got real good, she whispered plans to leave her husband and runaway with Devonte. His naivety and her beauty made him blind to the truth.

Was it all a lie?

Did she ever love him?

More importantly where would he go?

After waiting a little longer, he sat patiently for the waitress to return. He wanted to make eye contact with her. He didn't have money for the bill, he expected his lover to pay but she betrayed him.

Now he had different plans.

When the waitress finally glanced his way, Devonte stood up and moved toward the door. He wanted her to see what he was preparing to do. She made her assumptions anyway and he might as well prove her right.

"Hey, you gotta pay for your food!" she screamed running in his direction.

Instead of stopping, he pushed it open and strolled outside.

"Call the police!" she yelled pointing at the door. "That nigga didn't pay!"

PART TWO

And They Call Me God

PRESENT DAY

After telling them what she knew about Devonte's younger years, Samantha wiped her face, smearing some of the dried blood into long red streaks with the pressure. Taking a deep breath she sighed and said, "I don't know much about his past. Anything else I learned I got from the one he couldn't really possess. The one who held back some of herself, as if she were spoon-feeding him her love teaspoon after teaspoon."

"Was it Tykisha?" June asked, her eyebrows squishing together.

Samantha laughed. "You can't be serious." She took a puff of her cigarette, sending smoke into the air. "Do you know anything about Devonte? Or did you just take notes from the outside, without caring about his real story?"

June rolled her eyes. "You know the answer to that."

"How would I?" Samantha said through clenched teeth. "I know nothing about who you really are."

She took another puff of her cigarette and June secretly wanted to slap it out of her mouth. Not only did she stink of sex, alcohol and blood, but the smoke was drying out her eyes. Instead she kept her hands to herself and in frustration, June leaned back into the wall. "Well who was his first love?"

"He had many women, some before he was old enough to know what a woman really was. But there was one above all who had his heart. One that he

By T. Styles 63

would've given anything for if she just tried a little harder."

"Her name?" June asked, tiring of the games.

"Think," Samantha said taking slight pleasure of having information they didn't. "Use your imagination. Consider the cast of people who always surrounded him. If you try hard enough the answer will be clear. But here's a clue," she said in a condescending tone. "It wasn't me."

CHAPTER TWO

And Things Must Change

Summer, 1995

Fifteen-year-old Lauren Fletcher sat on the porch of her parents' house, a beautiful six-bedroom mansion surrounded by huge oak trees in rural West Virginia. With its pitted cerise colored greco and grey stones around the perimeter, it spoke to the power of the occupants who possessed it.

Money was in that house.

Accustomed to the best life had to offer, Lauren waited patiently for her boyfriend, Langston, to tell her what was so urgent it couldn't wait. In baited breath, she placed a strand of her long brown hair, seduced with locks of curls behind her ear and gazed at him with her worried green eyes.

In the background she could hear her horses prancing among the rocks and neighing.

Langston's handsome face contorted in anger as he took a deep breath and sighed. "I don't want to do this to you," he said softly. "I don't want to do this to *us*...but it's over."

She smiled, believing her ears were deceiving her. She may have chosen to play dumb, but her heart received the information correctly and responded in kind, by releasing several streams of tears down her face. "Langston...what...I'm...confused."

She swatted the tears away.

"It's over, Lauren and I know that you heard me."

Her neck bent forward. "But you...you said you would never do anything like this to me. You promised. So how can you sit there and break my heart?"

His Adam's apple bobbed as he swallowed and tried to prevent himself from choking up. "I'm protecting you, Lauren," he whispered as he looked toward the door and back at her. "I wish I could say more but I can't. I will tell you this...I'm not the man you think I am. I never was and never will be."

"What does that mean?" she asked...voice wavering.

He exhaled and leaned back in the chair. "I lied to you. I'm not in college and I don't work for the bank." He looked out at the driveway at his late model Mercedes. "Everything you think I am is wrong."

There was a tingling sensation in her chest. "Then what are you?"

"The kind of man you had no business dealing with," he said firmly. "Beautiful, I'm trying to tell you that I'm an eighteen-year-old hustler."

Her eyes widened. "Don't say that," she whispered. "If my parents hear you they won't let us be together." She looked at the screen door and back at him. "Plus I've been to the bank. You showed me where you worked. Remember?"

"It was all a lie, Lauren! Did you ever go inside? Just once?"

She stood up. "No, but I saw you come out."

"But did you see me at my desk, Lauren?" he yelled, angry she was so naive. He wanted her to be stronger not weaker for the next man.

"I don't care what you are, Langston. I don't care what you do for a living; all I ask is that you not leave me. We can make it work we just need a little time to clear things up that's all."

"There's no clearing shit up! It's over, Lauren. And I'll never see you again."

Realizing all was lost she said, "My father warned me to stay away from you and I should've listened." She spit in his face. "I will never disobey him again."

He smiled. "Now the real Lauren is coming out. The one who isn't green for real, but just plays the part."

"You don't know shit about me."

"I know you a hustler's wife. I know you know more than you let on."

"My daddy will bury you once he hears this shit," she said, having no real intentions on telling her father. The pain she felt had her spewing out all kinds of things. "He told me not to trust you and now look. He's always right."

She moved for the house as he broke out into laughter. "So that nigga throws me up under the bus and makes himself look like a saint." He shook his head. "I ain't even surprised."

She turned around and looked down at him...nostrils flaring. "Don't talk about my father."

"While you so busy putting him on a pedestal know this, your pops put me in the game. Who you think is my connect?" he laughed. "Your daddy. I was trying to hide you from this shit but what you not 'bout to do is act like he better than me."

He looked at her trembling body.

"Now your pops asked me to break up with you on account of some shit he caught up in. You 'bout to leave this house, Lauren. You moving out of the country, and he didn't want you to be mad at him for taking you away from me. The dream is over and it's all because he fucked over the wrong niggas...some dealers from Mexico. And now it's time to pay the piper, baby."

She shook her head rapidly from left to right. "No...it's not true! This is my house and my daddy is a doctor."

He laughed. "And what do doctors give patients to make them feel better?" he paused. "Drugs."

As if in slow motion, suddenly a blacked out six passenger van rolled up in front of the house. The side door slid open and despite the sunny day, five armed men, dressed in ski masks and hoods spilled from the vehicle as if they had been skiing the slopes. With automatic assault weapons in hand, they rushed the house aiming at Lauren and Langston.

With all hell breaking loose, Langston covered Lauren's body with his own, a true testament of his love. As glass from the house windows sprinkled on top of them like heavy balls of hail, she was mortified. Although she was concealed, the thunderous sound of their feet running up the wooden steps rocked her core.

What do they want? She thought.

"Langston...what's happening?" she whispered as his body felt heavier on her. "I'm scared."

He didn't answer.

He couldn't if he wanted to.

He took a long deep exhalation and as she lay under him, she could feel the warm blood from the bullet he took to the gut spilling onto her body. He was dead.

She could hear gunfire streaming from inside the house. Her muscles ticked as she battled with running, playing dead or entering the house to help her parents. When she heard her mother's screaming voice followed by her father's, the house fell eerily silent.

And They Call Me God

No more bullets ringing or pleas.

Slowly the men poured out of the house, three of them moved toward the van and one remained behind. Through the slits of her closed eyes she saw butter colored skin surrounding his large beady eyes. She would never forget them for as long as she lived.

He pointed the gun at Langston's back, and shot him again before rushing toward the waiting van. It wasn't until they pulled off that she prodded Langston's body off of hers. Standing up, soaked in blood, she wailed into the light blue sky.

Her life would never be the same.

5 YEARS LATER

The black plastic trash bag that sat on Lauren's legs made the tops her legs sweat as she rode the rocky bus to the Laundromat. Her fake leather purse leaning against her thigh didn't help to make her any cooler, but the bus was packed. She had to keep her belongings close so that others could have space to sit. And as she watched the landmarks speed past she felt frustration resting on her heart.

Her line of work wasn't something she ever envisioned for herself but it was honest. Unlike some of her stripper neighbors, she had a unique business that netted her a little cash. She washed and folded the clothing of local drug dealers for money. Her life was uneventful. If she wasn't in college, she was working.

As she was deep in thought, a chick wearing a tight red sweaty mini skirt played the hit song *"Get It On Tonite"* by Montell Jordan too loudly in the headphones of her Discman as she danced in place. Every time she moved, the body heat coming off her leg pressed against Lauren's forcing her into a quiet rage.

Lauren's laundry business started as a friendly gesture. Her next-door neighbor, who was a single drug dealer, would give her extra cash to buy his and her groceries. In return she would cook his meals and wash his clothes in the laundry room downstairs in their building. She accepted the offer and when he boasted to his friends at how good she cooked, and how he didn't need a girl to take care of him because he had Lauren, his friends were interested in the beautiful domestic cutie.

Bids were made to try to make her their girl but after losing Langston, she wasn't interested in a relationship and shot them all down. Instead she took their money and moved her laundry business to a Laundromat. Before long Lauren had ten regular customers who would give her collectively about one thousand dollars a month— enough for her bare basics.

At one point she stopped her business venture after meeting Varro, her ex-boyfriend. She met him while enrolled at the University of Maryland for equine studies…the study of horses in training for races. He owned a few horses himself in Virginia and wanted to learn how to breed, so he took a few courses, one of which she was a student in.

Although Varro was handsome with his light skin and hazel eyes…she avoided him because she liked him too much. And the more he pushed an introduction between them, the more she strayed away. After Lauren's entire family was killed and she was thrown from grace, a man was not in the cards for her but Varro was diligent. When he saw she was uncomfortable with his advances, he eased up on the flirting and made moves to help her succeed with her dream.

In disguise as a friend, Varro took her to his home, showed her his horses and she was in heaven. She rode them, took care of them and loved them. Always attracted to older men, in time she and Varro built a stronger connection. After a little more time, he seduced her young mind with money and power and she was in a trance.

They spent hours talking about his career in real estate and she spoke about her love of horses. In the end he gained her trust and attempted to win her over. Before saying yes she needed to know that he was being honest about his lifestyle, fearing she would give her heart to another drug dealer. She wasn't about to play a fool like she did with Langston.

Not only did she make him take her to his office, Varro Realty, she went inside and met his employees. Everything seemed legit and she agreed to spend the rest of her life with him. Slowly he convinced her to give up her side gig of washing clothes for other niggas, so that she could focus all of her attention on him, school and their horses.

In return she was given luxurious jewels, expensive clothing and a brand new Mercedes Benz. Before long she was back on top of the lavish lifestyle, where she was accustomed. She was addicted to the good life, so she moved into his mansion in suburbs of Virginia.

But her addiction had limits and she proved them to herself one sunny afternoon. She had just returned from a New York City shopping spree fully funded by Varro. Lauren shut the boutiques down, purchasing Christian Louboutin, Hermes, Celine and more. Money was no obstacle because Varro took care of her financially. It was as if she was in a dreamland when she was with him and every day was her birthday. She felt on top of the world until she overheard a conversation.

As she walked into the house, humming "Fortunate" by Maxwell, she dropped her shopping bags by the door and strolled into the kitchen. Easing off her chocolate fur coat, she tossed it on the back of the chair and grabbed a glass to pour her water in.

She smiled when she heard Varro yelling, knowing his tendency to scold his agents who failed to buy or sell homes properly. But when she heard the word cocaine she stumbled backwards into the refrigerator. The glass shattered at her Balenciaga pumps.

Hearing the noise, he walked into the kitchen and hung up on the caller. Staring into her green eyes, he knew in that moment he lost her. He placed the cordless phone on the counter. "Baby, let me explain," he said walking closer. "It's not what it sounds like."

"Who are you?" she asked trembling.

"It wasn't what you think," he continued, as the glass on the floor crunched under his footsteps. He reached out to her. "I was just talking to my man about—"

"Who the fuck are you?" she yelled as she slapped his hand away.

He exhaled, looked down at the floor and back into her green eyes. "I'm a dealer." He raised his arms and dropped them by his sides. "And I know you knew that."

The room felt as if it was spinning and she placed her hands on the counter for balance. *What's wrong with me?* She thought. *How come I keep attracting this kind of man?*

"I can't do this, Varro! You stood in this house and promised me that you weren't involved in that shit!

But you lied! I told you what happened to me! I lost everything because of the game! Everybody I loved! You fucking lied and I'm leaving you."

She grabbed her Louis Vuitton purse and moved quickly toward the door. At first his hands covered his face because this wasn't what he wanted. He cared about Lauren and felt that in time she would come to except his lifestyle. Of course the real estate company was nothing but a front to clean up his money and it was a good one at that. The plan was to explain it to her when she was so blind in love that she couldn't see straight. But now it looked as if that wouldn't happen.

As she moved toward the door, he snatched her by the arm and looked into her eyes. He parted his lips, preparing to beg harder, before closing them again.

"What the fuck you want, Varro?" she yelled.

Suddenly his posture grew perfect— shoulders back and neck exposed. "Fuck you think you going?" he asked slowly. "In *my* car?"

Her eyes widened and she placed her hand over her heart. "But you...gave it to me."

"With the drug money you claim you don't want," he reminded her before ripping the designer purse from her arm. "Everything you own belongs to me. I'll let you keep what's on your back, but the car and the other clothes in the closet stay here." He smirked. "I'll give it to another bitch who will appreciate it."

Her arms felt heavy. "I wish I never met you," she yelled.

"Don't fool yourself, youngin'," He laughed. "What you gonna do now? Go wash the draws of block soldiers who I own?" he paused. "Try finding another nigga with horses on his property. You will come back running and when you do I won't let your ass in."

So many tears welled in her eyes that she couldn't see straight. "All I wanted to do was take care of you. To love you."

"How you gonna take care of me, bitch? I was hardly ever home."

She looked around the house. "I loved it here."

"And you're giving it all up for nothing."

"Because I'm not for sale," Lauren said, storming out the house in tears. Having nowhere to go, she called on her long time friend Mario Hernandez. She met him years ago, after her parents were murdered, when they lived in a foster home together and became play brother and sister.

A year later, when they were both eighteen, Mario moved out and got his own place. With no strings attached he invited her to come live with him and she accepted. Because she was fragile, often crying for hours at a time, he didn't force his feelings on her. Although he had fallen in love with her a long time ago, he kept it a secret and after awhile he found himself in the friend zone with no relief.

When she left Varro, not wanting Mario to take care of her, she resumed her business and her clients couldn't wait to have her back. She was able to quickly get an apartment of her own.

When Lauren saw the Laundromat approaching from the bus, she stood up and pulled the cord ringing the bell to stop the bus. She discreetly tugged at her jean shorts, and pulled on her plain white t-shirt to allow air pockets into her chest to cool down from the heat. When the bus slowed she grabbed the bag and her purse and walked down the steps.

Once outside she walked toward the Laundromat, while receiving several honks from men thanks to the vivacious curves of her body. Although she wore fitting shorts and a plane t-shirt, Lauren wasn't attempting to grab attention. She wanted to be comfortable but the body she possessed wouldn't allow her to go unnoticed.

Once inside she placed her client's jeans in one washer, his whites in another and his coloreds in the last. With the clothing spinning, she grabbed her purse, removed a book and proceeded to read. She was on the best part of her book when Asher pushed open the glass doors leading into the Laundromat and rushed inside. It was as if he was running for his life.

Scared, she moved toward a large black folding table and hid under it as other patrons ran for safety too. Asher backed into washing machines in the far back of the Laundromat just as a tall handsome man wearing glasses so dark she couldn't see his eyes, entered.

It was Devonte Harrington.

Devonte was dressed in all black with a yellow gold chain dangling around his neck. At the base of the chain was a medallion that said GOD with so many diamonds you couldn't see the gold underneath. Behind him were three men— Shaw Kim, an immigrant from China who handled Devonte's real estate investments, Victor Greco, the son of a black whore and Italian mob boss who facilitated Devonte's block soldiers. And Chicago Swartz, a bomb specialist, who took pride in doing Devonte's bloodiest work.

Although not in all black, Devonte's men whom he called, The Triad, walked behind him as he moved closer to Asher. As Devonte advanced, what was most fascinating to all who observed was this clicking noise he made with his tongue. The tone was ominous and there was something terrifying about him.

"Please don't hurt me," Asher said with his hands pointed at the ceiling. Everyone in the Laundromat looked on, wondering if he would make it out alive.

"Why did you make me come in here?" Devonte asked calmly. "Why didn't you do what I asked?"

"I told them what you said, God," he responded shivering. "But some of them didn't listen." When Asher made an attempt to move Devonte clicked his tongue forcing him still.

Slowly Devonte turned his attention to The Triad. "Bring him to me."

Immediately Kim grabbed his left arm, Greco the right, while Schwartz hung behind them.

With several clicks of his tongue, Devonte walked up to Asher and placed his hands on the sides of his face as if he was a child. "I've shown you mercy but I'm getting tired. Really tired," he continued squeezing his cheeks so hard, that his teeth protruded forward and cut into the flesh of his inner jaw. "If you don't get those men off my blocks. *My blocks*," he said louder. "I will make you and everyone you care about pay." He released him and blood trickled out of his mouth and splashed onto the floor beneath his feet. "Now get out."

With his life in tow, Asher scurried away and Devonte turned around and preceded his clicking noises as he made his way toward the door. The Triad followed, where three gorgeous women stood next to the truck, two white and one black.

But when Greco saw Lauren crawling from under the table he walked toward her with a smile on his face...as if nothing happened. "Hey, beautiful," he said licking his lips. "When you gonna let me sweep you off your feet?"

And They Call Me God

"What I tell you about flirting with me," she said waving him off. "I have your jeans in the washer...don't make me bleach them," she joked.

He laughed and threw his hands up in the air. "You got it, mami. What were you doing on the floor?" he asked with his wide smile. Greco's black and Italian heritage made him so attractive some women found his looks offensive. Realizing a man that fine could do nothing but break hearts, they handled him carefully.

"I didn't know if...you know..." she pointed at the place Asher ran.

He smiled. "That ain't about nothing, just business." He looked at a washer that contained his blue boxers. "Damn, girl. I didn't know you did my clothes in this flea bag ass joint."

Lauren still shaken up by the scene could barely contain herself. "It's actually the best one in the city." She looked at Devonte who was easing into the back of a black Suburban. "Who is that?"

Greco looked at Devonte and back at her. "That's God...why?"

She frowned. "You call him God?"

"It's his name," he said seriously. "Everybody calls him God."

"Well he seems scary to me," she said pulling one of the washing machines open.

"Only if you have beef with him." He joked before looking at the washer again. "But look, ma, I gotta go. Just wanted to say thanks for doing what you do." He winked and walked toward the exit. "Hit me when they're done." He continued as he disappeared.

In that moment she felt like a maid as she moved his wet boxers to the dryer. Trying not to cry, she closed her eyes and envisioned the bigger plan. To own a ranch, live an honest life and have a family of her own. But first things first...so she placed quarters in the dryer and let them roll.

Lauren and Mario were in his apartment sitting on the sofa drinking vodka out of tiny glass cups. It was a modest one-bedroom crib that was dressed in the usual bachelor fashion— projection screen floor model TV, leather sofas and other furniture in all black.

As always she leaned on the side of his body while his arm draped around the back of her neck as they gazed at the tropical fish in his large tank. "Do you ever get lonely?" Lauren asked.

She reached down to grab one of her throbbing feet to massage it lightly. After washing, folding and ironing Greco's clothing earlier, which sat in clean bags by the door, she went to Mario's to chill.

"Lonely?" he asked as he looked down at her wanting to do nothing more than suck her toes. Mario was a full blood Latino and way too handsome to be single...but yet he was.

"Yeah...outside of me I never see you with any bitches," she looked up at him with her green eyes glistening. "So I want to know if you get lonely."

He shrugged, stood up and removed the empty glass that sat on the table in front of them. "Loneliness is relative."

She sat up, pulled her knees toward herself and rubbed her sore toes. "Meaning?"

He shrugged again and placed two ice cubes into her cup and three into his. "I want to spend my life with someone...the right person. But until that comes along I'm going to wait. So when I compare loneliness to what I really desire, I think I'm doing okay. Plus I have strong company in you."

She giggled. "Well what would she look like?" she asked excitedly. "Your dream girl?"

He handed her a drink and sat in the black recliner, a few feet away from her. She was always snuggling up against him, which drove him up a wall. It wasn't because he didn't want to sit next to her, but every time she played with her sore feet, which was often, his dick stiffened. Her cute little toes were more attractive to him then her plump ass and ample breasts.

As he considered her question, he wanted to say that his fantasy woman looked like her. And yet he didn't want to scare her off— he played the friend game so long he didn't want to look like a fraud. In his mind when all of the niggas fell by the wayside he would be there...waiting to sweep her off her feet.

"I don't know how she physically looks," he said sipping his drink before placing it on the table. He ran his hand through his coal black curly hair. "But I know she'll have to be loving, independent, smart and driven."

"Sounds like me." she laughed.

Silence.

When she felt his strong stare she cleared her throat and said, "Do you know somebody called God in Baltimore?"

Not feeling like talking about another nigga, he grabbed his drink and sat back. "Yeah...why? "

She let out an impatient huff, as if she'd wanted an answer for a minute. "Because I saw him rush up to some dude in the Laundromat today," she gazed into the living room as if replaying the moment. "I thought he was going to kill him but when he didn't, I was more scared of him."

By T. Styles   79

Mario examined her closely. He wasn't sure, but something told him she was far from afraid. She appeared enamored. Anyway, the last thing he felt like doing was talking about another man but the friend zone didn't exclude the topic. In order to keep the lie alive he had to talk about anything she wanted. "I know a little about him. Why? You want me to introduce you?"

Although Mario had a full time job as a mechanic, at one point he was involved in the darker side of life so he knew the underlings. But he made an escape just before things got out of control. So the street thugs respected him as Mario the Mechanic...nothing more and nothing less.

"No...he was just interesting to watch." One of her feet fell from the couch and she rocked it slightly. "He kept making this clicking noise with his mouth. Why?"

How he wished she'd change the questions back to him. "He does that shit to freak niggas out. He runs the Harrington Family... and they actually tried to get me to work for them a year ago." He looked away from her and at his fish. His jealousy was making his forehead throb. "Lauren, on the real, you'd do well to stay away from dudes like that. He's bad news and I hear he exploits women. You keep your mind on school and..." When he glanced over at her he was surprised that she was asleep.

Since the gabfest was over, Mario sat his glass down, stood up and moved toward the sofa. For a moment he looked down at her as if he were a stalker who was admiring her from a far. Her soft snoring gave him permission to stare harder than he would in her waking hours.

First he glanced at her feet, then her bare legs that were toned and smooth. Finally his gaze rolled on her belly and her beautiful face. Her long hair was directed in a soft bun and he tickled it a few times until it unraveled and fell along her face.

Licking his lips he bent down and carefully picked her up, like he had many times before. Slowly he walked her to his room and laid her in the middle of his bed. She was still snoring, except louder, which meant she fell deeper into sleep.

Unlike in the past when he would leave her alone, he eased behind her and unzipped his pants, as if they were about to have sex. He removed his long, thick, stiff penis and jerked it a few times as he eyed the curves of her body. Mario imagined that he was inside of her fleshy core, and she had her hands wrapped around his back, clawing at his skin, leaving bloody trails along the way.

When his imagination got the best of him, and he envisioned his head was nestled between her legs as he sucked on her pussy, he squirted nut into his hands. It felt so good that he didn't notice she stopped snoring.

Slowly she turned her head toward him — her facial expression blank. Since a sheet didn't cover him he was mortified. If she looked down at his hand she would see the levels of desperation he reached to keep his admiration a secret. If she saw him, he was certain that their friendship would be over.

Instead, still sleepy, she kissed him on the lips and said, "Thanks for taking care of me." She turned her head back around and snored quietly again. Luckily for him she hadn't bothered to lower her gaze...she was too exhausted.

"I gotta leave this girl alone," he said to himself. Sighing in relief he got his freaky ass out of the bed and took a cold shower.

Lauren stayed over Mario's like she normally did when they spent long hours together talking about life. Easing out of bed, she sat on the edge for a moment, yawned and walked toward the bathroom. When she opened the door she saw a fresh towel and washcloth on the linen table. Under them was a clean pair of Mario's sweat pants and a white t-shirt.

Under the pile was also a pair of his boxers but unlike the other clothes he left, he wore the boxers last night after his cold shower. This morning he took them off and folded them so that she wouldn't know. Just thinking about her pussy being somewhere his dick had been turned him on. Even if she sniffed the boxers she would never know he wore them because they still smelled fresh.

When she saw the love he put into taking care of her, she grinned and took a hot shower. And then for some reason a flash of Devonte entered her mind and she shook her head.

Why do you haunt me? She thought.

He was everything she knew she should steer clear of but she'd been intrigued and horrified by him at the same time. To the point where her pussy juiced up while she ran the washcloth within the folds of her vagina. With Devonte on her mind she allowed herself to cum in Mario's shower and instead of feeling ashamed, she felt relief.

When she was done she thought about her best friend. Although Mario wasn't her type she didn't know why. Unconsciously Lauren was attracted to a harder dude and Mario didn't meet her standards. He was too passive and in her opinion she'd run all over him. But if she could see herself as his woman she would've chosen him a long time ago. He was ride or die for her and she was certain he'd never hurt her feelings. But the idea of them being together stayed in the background, never being mentioned by either of them.

After she showered she walked into the living room where Mario was sleeping peacefully on the sofa. She slid up to him, lowered her body and kissed him on his warm cheek. He arose as if he were sleeping beauty and gazed into her eyes. She smiled down at him and said, "Thanks for the fresh clothes."

He grinned thinking about his underwear. With a serious face he asked, "You got the boxers too right?"

She pulled down the front band of the sweat pants and showed him the Hanes symbol. At first his dick jumped thinking he was about to get a glimpse of her pussy.

"Yep..." she winked. "And for your hospitality I'm going to cook you breakfast."

As she walked over to the refrigerator he watched her ass that jiggled even under his clothes. He wanted them boxers back dirty the moment she was done. Pulling the fridge's door she said, "Damn, Mario ain't shit in here." She frowned and closed it before moving over to her purse. "I'm gonna walk to 7-Eleven right quick and grab some eggs, salsa and bacon." She tossed it over her arm.

He stood up. "Nah...let me take you. You don't need to be walking when I got a car."

"I'm good," she said playfully hitting him on the arm. "Plus I haven't worked out today and could use the exercise." He was still moving toward his car keys. "Mario, it's only up the block."

He observed how sexy she looked in the basic clothing and imagined a million niggas trying to get at her. But he told himself they were friends and friends rarely contested. Besides, what was he going to say? *I don't want you to go because I don't want nobody trying to get at the pussy that I don't even own?* Instead he said, "Aight. Whatever you want."

Lauren was heading back to Mario's after buying the food and snacks she knew he liked. Before leaving Mario's house earlier, she told Greco that he could pick up his clothes from her there. The call came in at the right time because he was going to a club later and needed fresh gear.

As she walked down the block, a pair of headphones covered her ears that were connected to the CD player in her purse. She was playing *"Say My Name"* by Destiny's Child on repeat, and trying to get to the apartment before Greco did.

When she reached a flashing pedestrian walk sign, she waited for the signal to proceed. Just then a white Yukon blocked her path— the front tire spilled on the curb, inches from her foot.

Her heart dropped.

It was Varro and he had no respect for the law or her safety.

"Get in the car, Lauren," he said as he eyed the clothing he was sure belonged to another man. It had been six months since they'd broken up and he was angry with her for successfully moving on. Most

And They Call Me God

women would've been back on bended knees after having been given the world.

Not Lauren.

She glanced at the truck and then looked away really quickly, trying to pretend she didn't see him. When the sign changed she walked around the front of the vehicle and toward Mario's. She snatched the headphones off her ears and tossed them into her purse, figuring it was best to pay attention.

Feeling disrespected, all six-foot-five inches of Varro climbed out of the truck and towered over her shorter frame. "Did you hear what the fuck I said?" He grabbed her arm, forcing her to drop the bag in the middle of the crosswalk.

She snatched her arm away, picked up the bag now filled with cracked eggs and said, "Get back into your truck, drive to the bridge and go over the edge, nigga! I'm done with you!" She balled up her fist, hit him in the middle of the chest and stormed off. Although her heart thumped like a Texas drum major, she didn't let him know she was afraid.

Varro didn't heed her warning right away. Instead he stood in the middle of the street with a wide stance, watching her walk away. Finally when a bus beeped him out, he rolled his eyes at the driver and stomped toward the truck before getting inside and pulling off.

Lauren on the other hand hustled toward Mario's apartment quickly. She didn't like the way he looked at her and sensed danger. When she made it onto the street in front of Mario's building, Mario opened the window five floors up and looked down at her.

Smiling he said, "Damn, Lauren! You got me in this bitch hungry as shit!" he laughed. "'Bout time you came back." But when he saw the horror on her face the joke was over. "What's wrong?"

"I'll tell you in a second," She said trembling.

That was the first time Varro had approached her since the break up and up until that point she thought he moved on. Learning that he didn't after all this time made her feel queasy.

Impatiently she waited for the walk sign. When it changed she entered the crosswalk just as Varro's truck came from the right and smacked into her. Lauren's body flew up in the air, slammed into the grille of Varro's vehicle before sliding to the ground. There was so much blood that she was unrecognizable. Everything in the bag was on the ground— the eggs smashed into the concrete.

Mario screamed as he saw Varro grinning, before pulling away, with her blood on his truck.

And They Call Me God

CHAPTER THREE

When Things Come To Past

Naked, Stanford stepped into his expensive black marble-tiled bathroom in Baltimore, while Ninny Mashers—a cute 5'4 inch albino with a big ass and larger heart, slathered Albolene cream over his body. The product helped open his pores and allowed sweat to flow and as a professional MMA (Mixed Martial Arts) fighter, he had to make the weight or lose the payout.

His body and mind were a long way from what it use to be at Dove's Home For Boys. Then again a lot was different. After Devonte sexually assaulted him and Stanford was remanded to a psychiatric center, by all accounts he had gone mad.

Being raped by another man did things to him psychologically he couldn't grapple. Most importantly it had him questioning his identity. Not knowing were to place the anger, he turned on his cousins and isolated them from his life. And when he was finally deemed sane after not talking for over two years, he was old enough to go out on his own.

Harper and Wayne didn't fair any better in the world, the criminal underbelly that was Baltimore, sucked them into a vacuum of hell and hate. Forcing the cousins to look at people and their possessions as objects and prey. Simply put, if you had what they wanted, they took it.

Although Stanford and his cousins led parallel lifestyles after Dove's, neither knew about the status of the other. And it was how Stanford wanted it. The less people he had around him the clearer the mind.

Angry at the world he took up mixed martial arts boxing and was the best Baltimore had to offer. Before long he became muscle for a few dealers who wanted to make money without the risk associated with not having protection. He grew stronger and angrier and women couldn't appeal to his inner spirit.

Besides, he didn't know what he wanted.

Fucking them violently, he would often send them on their way without so much as a return call. Clueless, at first he thought he was homosexual but when he stepped into a gay bar to test the theory, he was so disgusted that he ran out ten minutes later and vomited at the entrance.

And then he met Ninny at a gym a year later.

Everything changed.

Ninny helped out a lot around the gym where he trained and was good at what she did. When the men got banged up in the ring, she knew the skills necessary to repair them. She was also skilled at what it took to help fighters make goal weight for boxing matches.

That's how she and Stanford connected.

Like Stanford, Ninny didn't speak much. Receiving flack most of her life for her extra light complexion and gold hair due to albinism, she always felt out of place. But Stanford saw her inner and outer beauty and after time she started caring for his career exclusively. In his life her experience was priceless and a few boxers grew angry when she wouldn't help them anymore, so the two of them left the gym and continued his boxing career elsewhere.

One night Stanford was hammered in a fight. There was so much blood covering him that Ninny could barely see his eyes. He was in excruciating pain but he'd also won the match and deserved to be rewarded.

Laying on the floor in his dressing room, Ninny figured he needed something else that was not in a bottle. Without there ever being a mention of them being together, she lowered his boxers, pulled down her jeans and her panties before sliding on top of him and riding his stiff dick.

Stanford learned two things in that moment as Ninny fucked him swiftly and carefully. First...he was not gay, second that he was in love. Ninny was his caregiver, his bitch and his biggest supporter. And after the past he had he needed her more than he realized. They became an item and there was no turning back. Their relationship, nurtured in silence but bathed in love was unwavering.

After bucking his gun a few more times for pay, he gave up the goon life and decided to put all of his attention into the MMA career and his woman.

After she smeared the Albolene on his skin, she helped place all 182 pounds of him into a rubber sauna suit to raise his body temperature. Naked, pussy out and titties swinging, she sat in the sauna with him, as he gazed into her eyes, falling deeper in love.

When he was done sweating all he could, she filled a hot bath with 8 pounds of Epsom salts and 10 pints of isopropyl rubbing alcohol, to pull more water from his body. Removing the suit, he eased inside the water and Ninny knelt next to the tub, stroking his hand.

After the bath, thirty minutes later he staggered out of the tub and Ninny placed him back into his sauna suit. When he was ready she put hot towels over his body. Kissing him passionately while he waited, twenty minutes later she helped peel off the suit. Sweat poured from his skin like a waterfall and they both grinned.

By T. Styles   89

They knew their process was successful.

Later that day Stanford went to the gym and successfully weighed in at 170 pounds. Excited, she jumped into his arms and celebrated.

During the professional bout, two days later, he beat a man so badly his jaw dislocated and he entered a coma. While Ninny went to collect the winning payout, Stanford accepted a call from one of his clients, Asher in his dressing room.

"Thanks for taking my call man," Asher said. "I didn't want to bother you with this shit but I'm losing my blocks."

Stanford rested the phone on his bloody shoulder. "And?" he continued removing the wraps from one of his hands.

"*And* this nigga is gonna take me out of business if I don't get help." He responded passionately. "You the only person I know who's time enough for a dude like this."

When Ninny strolled into the dressing room, she smiled and showed him the check for $76,000.82— his winnings for the evening. He grinned and slapped her ass.

Still turned on from how he beat his opponent and won the fight, she placed the check down and sat on the dresser in front of him with her legs open. He could feel the heat from her pussy and couldn't wait to get into her plushy center later. Although they fooled around, sex was out of the picture pending the fight...now it was over. While winking, she took over removing the bandages leaving him to his call.

"Are you still there man?" Asher asked.

"Yeah...but I don't work in that line of business anymore," he said.

"But I need your help," he replied breathing heavily. "Come on, man. I'll pay your price. Whatever it is. Just get this nigga off my back."

Stanford looked up at Ninny and winked. "You not listening, Asher. I'm all about my fights now. I can give you a few tickets for my next bout but that's it."

Asher knew he was his last chance and felt defeated. He exhaled and said, "Well, I might as well go pick out my burial plot because this nigga Devonte is gonna end me."

When Stanford heard the name of the man who raped him his eyes widened. And Ninny, without explanation, knew something was wrong.

"What did you say his name was?" Stanford questioned, pushing the phone against his ear.

"God," Asher said thinking either name would suffice.

"No...you said something else," Stanford responded as he clenched his fist.

"Devonte?" Asher said unsure what the big deal was. If the nigga wasn't going to help him Asher was totally uninterested in playing twenty-one questions.

Stanford looked up at Ninny again. "Stay by the phone. I'll tell you where to meet me in a few days."

✝

Mario stabbed the third floor button so many times on the elevator's panel that his index finger throbbed from the pressure. As the car moved toward the top, he impatiently paced the floor. When he followed the ambulance earlier, they couldn't give him much information on her condition and he didn't know what to expect. More than anything he felt powerless as he couldn't do what was necessary to protect her.

Having a nervous reaction, he pinched at the skin of his throat until it bled before the elevator dinged and the doors opened. Once they did he sloshed into the hallway and moved hurriedly in her room's direction.

He panted heavily as he walked down the hall but when he saw three men with black hoods over their heads hanging outside of the room in an intimidating fashion, he was confused.

Who the fuck are they?

From where he stood he couldn't see their expressions but the whites of their eyes looked like ghosts in the darkness of their hoods. Mario's pace slowed until he was next to her room. He gazed inside and his heart broke when he saw her lying on the bed with her eyes closed, bandaged from head to toe.

Not feeling like introductions, he attempted to walk inside and received a firm shove to the chest by one of the men. The person maintained his hold until Mario pushed his hand down. "Get the fuck off me," he told him.

In response, the stranger gripped his collar and shoved him into the wall, lifting him off of his feet. "You not getting in, Spaniard. Now get the fuck out of my face."

Mario wiggled from his grasp and said, "You don't know me, nigga!" He wanted to wreck but the man's size was greater than his. "Now my friend is in there and I'm going inside."

Just then Varro walked outside of Lauren's room. "No you not," he said. "You gonna stay right out here." He had been sitting in a chair, obscured from view. Recognizing him from the window, he strolled up to Mario with a grin on his face. "You have to forgive Bo," he said pointing to the man who just lifted him off his feet. "He's not accustomed to hospitality like I am."

"What are you doing here?" Mario asked huffing and puffing. Facing the man who tried to kill her caused him to hyperventilate.

"I'm protecting my girl," he said calmly. "Somebody hit her and ran away from the scene. I'm just making sure she'll stay safe."

Mario's legs felt weakened but he maintained his stance. Dude perpetrating like he didn't know what happened to Lauren had him feeling violent. "Well I want to see her now."

Varro looked into the room. "Naw...it's not a good time." He looked back at Mario. "She's been given pain meds and is sleep anyway. Come back later. Unless you know who did it?"

Suddenly the three men surrounded Mario.

Mario looked up at them and said, "Naw...I don't know nothing." He gazed into Lauren's room again and made silent vows to return. "I'll be back. You can count on it." He wiggled between them and walked toward the elevator.

Varro watched him the entire time.

Greco hopped up the stairway leading to Mario's apartment to get his clothes from Lauren. When he reached the door he doubled checked the address written in his pocket before knocking.

When Mario opened the door Greco was surprised that he knew him and secondly that he looked so badly. It was as if life drained from his body and made him pale. "Mario?" Greco said looking him over. "You good, man?"

"Yeah...what do you want...I mean, what are you doing here?" he was so put off by Lauren's accident that he forgot Greco's clothing was in his apartment.

"Lauren said my stuff was here," he responded in an uncertain tone. "I came to get it."

Mario wiped his hand down his face as he finally remembered. "My bad, man. It's just that...well...Lauren's in the hospital."

Greco's eyebrows rose upon hearing the news. Lauren was his people and hearing that she was hurt was fucked up. As far as he knew she was a square and not in the fast life. "What happened? She good?"

"Somebody hit her in the middle of the street and ran," Mario started. He wanted to say more but he didn't know if he could trust him, or if he knew Varro.

"What the fuck? She need anything?" Greco asked honestly. "Whatever it is, it ain't a problem."

Mario twisted his hands together and rubbed them down the front of his pants. "I think I need to," Mario backed up and looked at Greco. Taking a deep breath he said, "Is the option still open to meet God?"

Greco shrugged. "I don't know...I mean he reached out last year and didn't take kindly to how you treated his offer. It may be hard to get him to come around."

"This is important. I wouldn't ask to see him if I had other options."

Greco nodded. "I'll see what I can do."

And They Call Me God

CHAPTER FOUR

Deals With The Worst Kind

In his penthouse apartment overlooking the Baltimore Inner Harbor, Devonte sat on his plush leather sofa. In front of him was a row of cocaine and small little H's on tiny individual papers. Just opposite of him sat The Triad— each with a beautiful woman with skin like chocolate, vanilla and butter pecan. On a table before them, sat six tiny red letter H's on small pieces of paper.

Directly above Devonte's head, stuck to the wall was a painting in a gold frame of a naked black woman with silver angel wings behind her. On the right side of him was Tykisha, on the left Heather and at his feet sat Samantha.

The three of them were the first to recognize Devonte's power. They all met in a group home years back and since each came from a violent background, they clicked instantly.

First there was Samantha Herrnstein who seemed to be taken by Devonte immediately. Although she was strikingly beautiful now, in the beginning she wasn't classically beautiful and looked harder than the others. Still there was something about her that appealed to him. She was a natural blonde with aqua blue eyes and a straight nose. Back then her pale white skin seemed to stretch over her bones too tightly giving her a mannequin like appeal. But he coaxed her insecurities and in turn gained her loyalty.

Then there was Heather Swenson who back in the day was messy but cute. When he first met her, she always wore her red hair on the right side of her face, as if deliberately revealing only half of herself at a time. But after Devonte got a hold of her heart and mind she wore her hair in a tight ponytail that hung down her back. With Devonte's love, she was done hiding from the world.

Lastly there was Tykisha Marlo. A pretty slender dark skin girl who back in the day isolated herself from the others in the group home. Although she gave him attitude, the first thing he noticed was her cute face and her sensual mouth that always shined with pink lip-gloss. She was seductive and glacial all at once and the one he felt the closest connection although they always butted heads.

"We are reaching a point where we must get stronger," Devonte said softly. "No more playing games out here with these niggas."

Over the years he had become stronger and more charismatic, knowing exactly what to say to get what he wanted. The drug lord of a small section of Baltimore, he ruled through power and fear and was effective.

"And to do that we must stay bonded allowing nothing to come between us." He continued. "Take the communion, and let us connect in ways others could only dream."

Each of them, with the exception of Devonte, picked up the sheets, and placed one small red H on their tongue. Although the letter stood for Harrington, it was LSD which he spoon-fed his subordinates on a regular basis. Having basic knowledge on psychedelic powers, he knew that if he fed them the drug continuously, and deposited his rules and outlook on life during the process, they would be devoted to him blindly.

And they were.

The Harrington family, a little over one hundred strong, bullied their way into the drug market in Baltimore. Before long they became a staple in the crime world but there was one block he wanted above all, for personal reasons. Although it was somewhat non essential, only netting a few thousand a day, he looked at as the Pacific Avenue property on a Monopoly board. He had the other properties and he wanted to complete the set.

Within seconds of the acid taking hold he told them how together they would always be successful. And after the brief speech, they experienced psychotic trips that were unworldly. He was killing their egos so that in the end, he would be the only person they needed.

When they were done with the communion, Devonte sat back and relaxed to the soothing sound of The Triad making love. Suddenly Heather, whose body Devonte etched out a few years ago, that included a tiny waist, wide hips and a large rear, lowered her body and rubbed her vagina over a row of cocaine. When she was done, she eased toward Devonte and he grabbed a fistful of her long hair before running his tongue along her neck. She climbed on top of his thickness and allowed her berry colored center to engulf his chocolate dick.

Tykisha and Samantha took an H tab each and fell back in a psychedelic haze while Devonte pulsated inside of Heather's body.

"I love you, God," Heather whispered as she rolled her hips. "So much."

Devonte flipped her on the stomach, spread her cream legs apart and rammed deeply into her sloppiness. She was in pain and in ecstasy, evident by the speck of blood that covered his penis.

By T. Styles   97

Samantha eyed them, wondering why she was never chosen first but always last.

He gripped her breasts and pinched her nipples so hard she begged him to stop but Devonte was anything but accommodating once he was in the pussy. He ignored her plight in an effort to please himself. And when he was done he rose up and walked to his bar.

As he poured himself a glass of whiskey, the sounds of the family fucking played behind him. Lovemaking noises were the only music he needed.

The warm liquor oozing down his throat reminded him of one thing...that he was bored with life. Outside of roughing up Asher, he didn't have the excitement he needed to give him passion. People were afraid of him and he needed action in his life.

But how?

The next day Devonte was sitting on his balcony, which overlooked the stunning view of the Baltimore Harbor. The cool breeze coming in from the horizon kissed the water and caressed his face as he inhaled the fresh air. Falling deeper into relaxation, he readjusted his shades and exhaled. He came a long way from living in a dirty apartment under the house at Myers.

The sounds of pots and pans knocking inside of the house alerted him that the girls were up and about to prepare breakfast. Although he enjoyed being with the family, he relished the moments alone where he could get his thoughts together.

And They Call Me God

When the door opened to the balcony Devonte said, "What's up, Greco?"

Greco laughed and closed the sliding door. "How do you do that? No who's behind you before they talk?"

Devonte shrugged and leaned back in his chair. "It's your energy."

Greco nodded and sat next to him before taking a look at the view. "I can see why you love sitting out here," He sighed and he inhaled deeply. "It's beautiful."

"Can you believe five years ago I had fifty bucks and no place to go?" Devonte paused. "And now we have all of this. More money than we could imagine, and so much pussy all we have to do is roll over and we're knee deep in it."

Greco smiled. "The worst thing they could've done was put us in that group home together." He paused as if trying to remember something. "What you get caught up for again?"

Devonte laughed. "Not paying for pancakes at IHOP." He shook his head. "Dumb shit."

Greco chuckled heartedly. "And they got me, Chicago and Shaw for holding up a convenience store with water guns." Greco gazed outward, as if he could see the memory clearly in the sky. "At that time it was only The Triad, you, Tykisha and Heather."

Devonte rested his right ankle on his left knee. "You forgot about Samantha."

"Damn, we always forget about her." Greco said softly. "We were just some nobodies the world gave up on back then. Until we rolled up on Money Making Coleekio. We held him down while you put that barrel to his head and squeezed."

"Got away with all his work and fifty thousand dollars in cash." Devonte whispered. "Left that group home and been together ever since."

"But now we're over a hundred deep."

"And still something is missing from my life," Devonte said out loud. "I'm so bored I can't stand myself sometimes." Done with the reminiscing he cleared his throat. "So when are you going to tell me what's on your mind? I felt it before the communion yesterday and I feel it now.

Greco eyed Devonte whose gaze remained outward. "It's really not that big of a deal."

He crossed his arms over his chest. "If it bothers you it's important to me."

Greco nodded. "Remember the girl I was telling you about...the one who does my laundry with the green eyes? Well, someone hit her in a truck and ran the other day. She's in a hospital fighting for her life."

Devonte turned toward him. "You want me to find out who it was?"

"No...it's not that," Greco said. "Her friend...wants to meet you."

His right eyebrow rose. "Who is her friend?"

"Mario...the mechanic you wanted to join the family last year."

Devonte leaned back and crossed his arms over his chest. Could this be the excitement he needed? "You mean the one who refused the invitation." He shook his head. "Now he comes back on bended knee."

Greco nodded yes. "Want me to tell him to beat it?"

Devonte was suddenly intrigued. What did the girl being hit and Mario meeting have to do with him? "No...I'm in the entertaining mood these days. Set the meeting up...I'll see what I can do."

"I didn't ask who the dude was in the truck that hit her. I can find out first if you want."

"Not necessary," Devonte said confidently. "Whoever it is, is no threat to me."

"Are you sure, God?"

Devonte nodded. "But I would like to know if he's been in contact with the Los Esqueletos recently?"

MARIO'S PAST

Mario stood in the middle of a huddle of teenagers as he was repeatedly assaulted in the face...upper and lower body. Blood gushed to the surface of his skin before the flesh was broken and it dripped to the ground. Instead of running, he accepted each jab as if it were as natural as breathing.

With all energy stolen, Mario doubled over, preparing to kiss the concrete when Hector A. Hernandez yelled, "That's enough!" The circle of abusers opened and Hector stepped up to Mario who was leaning on one of the men to maintain balance. A smile rested on Hector's face, because Mario took the initiation like a G. "I knew you were tough, cousin. But I'm impressed."

Mario smiled and Hector pulled him into an embrace as the others cheered.

"I'm just glad that shit's over," Mario said.

Hector snapped his fingers and he was handed a black hoodie with *Los Esqueletos* in white words across the front. He brought it down over Mario's blood soaked black hair, which caused extreme stinging as it brushed against his bruised skin. But when the shirt was on, when he finally looked down at the letters, Mario exhaled. After so long he was a member of the gang he had come to admire all of his life.

"Welcome, cousin," Hector pulled him into his slender frame. "You earned it. Well...almost."

Mario's excitement melted away. "So I'm not in?"

"Of course," he paused, "almost. When something is born...something else must die. In other words you can only be born into Los Esqueletos when you kill. Are you prepared to take the next step...because you have a choice now? Once you are a part of us...once you breathe as we do, there is no turning back."

Mario looked square at him, eyes gleaming and said, "I will do anything you ask. That's on my life."

Mario sat next to Hector in the back of an all black 1968 Buick Rivera, as Hector loaded a silver Smith & Wesson .357 while wearing latex gloves. The leather seats groaned every time Mario moved due to the aching sensation in his belly. Two other members of the Los Esqueletos, Felipe and Pablo, sat in the front, quietly, as if meditating upon the upcoming act.

When the bullets were loaded in the weapon, Hector handed Mario the gun along with an address on a small piece of paper. "Put all six slugs into him and then eat this paper."

"Eat it?" Mario repeated.

"Swallow it...no evidence," he smiled. Mario nodded but he didn't appear confident enough for

Hector. So Hector gripped his new gang member by the collar. "If you fuck this up, you can't come back."

"I know," Mario said, eyes wide before growing smaller.

"I don't think you understand what I mean...you fuck this up and you be better off saving a bullet to put one in your head.

The car slowed and Hector released him.

Mario took a moment to look down at the sheet...there was a number 8 and the name Axel written in red.

"That's the door number and that's his name," Hector said. "The building is right there," he pointed out of the window at a large project. "You do this and you're in." he looked deeper into his eyes. "You don't and well...you already know the deal."

Mario tucked the weapon in the front of his jeans and eased out of the car. He didn't bother to look back because he knew it would be perceived as weak. Instead he rushed toward the building, past a few onlookers as if he were a military soldier.

Once there he pulled open the glass door and to his surprise, on the far end of the same floor was apartment #8. He moved toward it gradually until the place where he was going produced a tall Hispanic male who was holding a kid's hand. The man gazed down at the child, while smiling— oblivious to Mario's attention.

The man closed and locked the door and was in the middle of the hallway when Mario yelled, "Axel!"

Axel's eyes widened as Mario cocked his gun and aimed.

"My son," Axel said softly as he looked down at the boy. "Please don't do this. I'm begging you."

Mario's arm stiffened and he aimed harder, his body trembling as the gun quivered. His arm relaxed and stiffened again before he reconciled with the fact that he was not a killer.

When a woman near where he stood opened her door, he aimed the gun at her and pushed inside her apartment. Afraid of rape, her worst fear, she screamed at the top of her lungs until he yelled, "Shut the fuck up! Just shut up! I'm trying to concentrate! I'm not here to hurt you!"

She placed both of her hands over her mouth and backed up into the wall. "Take what you want…just leave."

Mario stared at her momentarily, placed the gun on the counter and slowly picked up the handset. Tears rolled down his face because he knew that he had betrayed his favorite cousin…who was also a very dangerous man.

With the handset clutched in his palm he dialed 911 and reported a crime.

Against himself.

Mario never saw his cousin again, but he was certainly looking for him.

When there was a knock at Mario's door he gaped out the peephole and took a deep breath when he saw The Triad. The stance they carried let it be known that this was a business meeting with little potential for pleasantries. When he was ready to meet the man he ignored for the past year, taking a deep breath he pulled the door open.

Greco, Chicago and Shaw ripped through the small abode, checking for any threats on Devonte's life.

And They Call Me God

When they were satisfied that he would be safe Chicago walked outside and returned with Devonte who made clicking noises as he slowly ascended the steps.

Once in the doorway Devonte clasped his hands in front of his body and grinned. "Mario...so we finally meet." He stepped further inside and hung a few feet in front of him. "My only question is what the fuck do you want with me?"

Mario cleared his throat. "My friend...Lauren is in the hospital. The person who hit her has men guarding the room and he won't let me see her." He paused. "I'm worried that he'll kill her to prevent her from talking to the police. I know it's crazy but it's all I can say about it right now."

Devonte nodded. "So why should I get involved?" he shrugged. "When you made it clear you didn't want God's help."

Mario's feet moved a little under his body. "I just wanted to stay out of trouble," he paused. "I made a lot of moves to avoid the lifestyle that you're accustomed and —"

"Fuck you think you know about God?" Devonte roared causing Mario to cower a little. Like others, Mario was use to Devonte carrying a calm tone when he spoke and this mood was different.

"I'm sorry, Devonte. I didn't mean it like —"

"God," Devonte corrected him swiftly. "They call me God now."

Mario nodded not willing to call him God just yet, especially when he hadn't performed any miracles for him. "No disrespect intended," he said quietly. "But I wanted to stay out of gang related business."

"And now?"

His gaze fell on the floor before rising on Devonte. "Well now I'm willing to do whatever I must."

"You must really care about this girl."

"Yes…I do."

"So what do you want?"

"I need to see her and a place to put her for a few days," Mario responded as if he was speaking to the Wiz. "It doesn't have to be fancy…just undetectable."

Devonte adjusted his shades. "Once you make a deal with me there's no exit clause. You do understand this right?"

"Yes," Mario said softly. He took a deep breath. "That's why I didn't call you until I was sure."

Devonte exhaled. "I'll lend a few of my best to go with you to the hospital. And then I'll need a favor that will be payable at a later date."

"Whatever I have to do, I'm in."

Devonte sat in Aubrey Jenkins house as she prepared him breakfast—bacon, hash browns, cheese grits and homemade biscuits. Through the years they developed an unconventional relationship that worked for them but was too weird for others. It was built on virtually zero respect on Devonte's part.

When the food was done she placed a hefty plate in front of him and sat across from him. He grabbed his fork. "You not eating?"

She smiled. "Naw, boy. Like to see you get at it though. I'll probably thaw out the greens in the freezer later and eat them."

He stuffed his mouth, forkful after forkful. When he was done he sat his utensil down and said, "How come you won't tell me where that nigga is?"

"By nigga do you mean your father?" she asked shaking her head. "And my son?"

Silence.

"I won't tell you because you're angry," she continued. "And I'm afraid you'll hurt him."

"I don't have a right to be angry at a man who didn't do shit for his own kid?"

"Devonte, that ship has sailed. You're a grown man."

"God...they call me God now."

She waved him off. "And the only God I calls on is the one in my Bible," she responded playfully.

Devonte seemed heavy. "You never cared about me did you? Before my aunt asked you to come get me."

"I cared but look where I live, Devonte. In a subsidized building for elders. I have one bedroom that's almost as small as efficiency. I wasn't in a position to help." She observed him suspiciously. "But look at you now. You've done well for yourself."

"But it wasn't because of you," he roared. "You abandoned me...you left me on my own and I will never forget."

Aubrey sighed and sat next to him. "You call yourself God but do you think I'm immortal too?"

He frowned. "What do you mean?"

"Do you think I'm some majestical creature who can wield all sorts of power?" she paused. "If you do you shouldn't because just like you I am human, Devonte. I make mistakes and one of my mistakes caused you pain in your younger years. But like your aunt, I'm trying to make things right."

"You don't know what you talking about when it comes to her. She knew she was the only person I had and she rolled out on me anyway." He paused. "When she was high I cleaned her crusty wounds. And when I needed her she didn't return the love. Why should I agree to meet with her just because the guilt is eating her alive?"

"She's dying of cancer, Devonte."

"We're all going to die. At least she knows how."

Aubrey slapped him so hard it took almost a minute for the sting to go away. He stood up and laughed.

"Never put your hands on me again, old bitch," he said as if she were not his grandmother.

Aubrey trembled with rage as Devonte clicked his tongue and moved toward the window.

She looked upon him, as the stranger he appeared to be. "I don't have much, Devonte. As a matter of fact I have nothing." She paused. "But you're never going to have peace if you don't learn to forgive. You call yourself God but you know nothing of mercy."

"Tell that to the nigga I had under my boot. With a sawed off shot gun pressed to his forehead, that I allowed to live when he asked for mercy."

She shook her head. "What can I do to ease the pain you're in?"

He turned around and leaned against the window. "I'll let you know when I'm sure. This time don't refuse me."

Lauren was posted in the hospital bed with two broken legs and a broken arm. Boy was she miserable. Varro came to the room everyday with jewelry and so many flowers the room was potent with the burly stink of sweet roses. Although the three-armed men

And They Call Me God

remained posted outside of her room, today was the only day Varro hadn't shown up.

She wanted to leave to breathe the fresh air and take a shower in her own apartment. But earlier in the week she overheard Varro making arrangements to have her moved somewhere more secluded. He claimed he couldn't trust her not to go to the authorities, when in actuality he wanted to keep her for himself. And the accident gave him the perfect reason to kidnap her. Once she left the hospital she was certain that she would never be found again.

Mario was also on her mind and heart. She felt guilt when she considered how he witnessed her getting struck with Varro's truck. She knew he felt helpless and the look in his eyes before she went down would forever stay etched on his mind.

Realizing she would be stuck with Varro, she gazed at the only beauty around, the red roses across from her in the crystal glass. Sighing deeply, she tried her best to drift off to sleep.

Mario stomped up the hallway with Heather, Tykisha and Samantha following. He was pissed when Devonte told him he would lend his best arms only for three females to show up. But what could he do? As it stood he didn't have any help so he would have to take what he could or risk his and Lauren's life trying to get her away from Varro.

Although their makeup was done to perfection, their gear was basic. Dressed in black jeans and oversized men's grey hoodies, they worked the hallway like models on a runway. All three of them had their hair pulled back in tight ponytails revealing their faces fully. He felt like their hoodies were a little too large for their frames and then he had a moment of recollection. They were toting high-powered weapons.

As they moved closer, Mario could see Varro's goons push off the walls they were leaning against. And then something happened. The cocky looks Varro's men once possessed when Mario was alone, diminished.

They were fearful.

And when Mario and the Harrington ladies were directly in front of them, not only did they pull the black hoods off of their huge heads, they also placed their hands up in surrender.

Mario had to gaze back at the ladies to see if they were doing anything special to warrant such a reception. But when he did all he saw was the same blank expressions they wore from the start.

"We here for the girl," Mario said more confidently. "And we're not leaving without her."

"No problem," one of them said. "Do what you got to do. I'll just let V —"

"You'll call no one," Tykisha said as she introduced the hammer she was holding. It was a beautiful .45 revolver with a bullet for every hole in the chamber. Aiming in his direction she said, "You have God's permission to call whomever you like once we leave…but not before."

He nodded in understanding and leaned back against the wall with the others.

When Mario moved into the room, Lauren's solemn look brightened when she saw his face. She reached out for him with her good arm, and he ran toward her for an embrace. The way he held her, she could tell he was willing to die for her.

And They Call Me God

When they separated he said, "I'm gonna get you dressed. I'm taking you out of here."

"Mario, you don't understand...he won't let me alone," she warned. "I don't want you involved in any of this. Just leave me."

"Trust me, Lauren. I'll take you somewhere safe," he said confidently. When she didn't seem convinced he sat on the edge of the bed and caressed her hand. "I wouldn't be here if I wasn't willing and able to go the distance." He put his palm over his heart. "You just have to trust me."

Lauren looked out of her door at Varro's men. At first they wore smug expressions but now they resembled three alter boys.

"Okay, Mario," she said looking into his eyes. "If you're sure then I'll trust you."

Aubrey placed an apple pie on the table where Devonte, Lauren and Mario sat on the sofa of her tiny apartment. Lauren was propped up on the end with her legs on a chaise so she would be comfortable. The trio had just finished a meal of fried chicken, mac and cheese and green beans and they were stuffed.

Although the hospitality was at an all time high, Lauren's gaze remained on Devonte most of the time. She was trying to figure him out. He pretended to ignore her, only speaking to her through Mario, but she could tell that he was as intrigued by her as she by him. She never met a man that amused and scared her at the same time.

"Come on, Ms. Aubrey," Mario said rubbing his belly. "We've been here for two days and you've been stuffing us like crazy. I think we're done for the night."

Lauren grinned. "Yeah, Ms. Aubrey, I already gained seven pounds." She paused as she felt tears about to brew. "I'm just so grateful. I know you don't know me, but letting me stay here is not only restoring my faith in people, but it's giving me hope that I'll get through this okay."

As they joked with his grandmother Devonte thought about what happened to him when he needed help as a child. Instead of a warm couch and a hot meal he was shipped off to Dove's Home For Boys. He wasn't trying to be resentful but the bitter pill was hard to swallow.

He would've never humored asking her to let them stay if it wasn't for the boredom that ate at him on a continuous basis. Who was Lauren and why was she worth fighting for? Devonte was also jealous of Mario and his ability to love Lauren from a far despite it not being returned. So he asked to let them hold up and in turn promised his grandmother a new crib.

She wasn't going to accept his offer but their overnight presence in a building for elders could cause her to get put out, and she was horrified of being homeless.

When there was a knock at the door Aubrey rushed toward it, looked out of the peephole and looked back at them. "Be quieter," she whispered fearfully.

She opened the door very little so that the person couldn't see them inside, "Hey, Naomi. What you need?" she closed the door a little more.

"What I need?" she joked. "Let me in silly woman and I'll tell you," she said from the hallway.

And They Call Me God

Aubrey looked away as if trying to gather her thoughts before focusing on her again. "I can't right now."

Naomi poked her tongue into her inner cheek. "What...for the first time since I've known you, you have a man over?"

Just then the Motorola cell phone in Devonte's pocket rang. He removed it, answered and was given bad news. The men on Asher's blocks had not gone and it was time to escalate matters.

Unable to hear the conversation between his grandmother and Naomi anymore he rose from his seat and walked toward the door. Pulling it open he said, "Listen you nosey, bitch. She doesn't want to invite you into her home. If and when she does she'll let you know." He slammed the door in her face.

Aubrey was so embarrassed that she took several breaths to regain her composure. She leaned against the door. "You don't have any respect for anyone do you? I knew you had problems with me but that old woman never did anything to you." She looked drained and scared.

"You not gonna be here much longer," Devonte said. "You going to a place where you don't have to kiss somebody's ass."

Embarrassed, Aubrey sighed and said, "Well...who wants ice cream?" she walked into the kitchen without an answer.

Lauren was angry. "You really shouldn't talk to your grandmother like that."

Devonte didn't reply.

Instead he clicked his mouth a few times, walked toward Mario and tapped him on the shoulder. They eased toward the window out of earshot of everyone. "I'm cashing in my favor."

Mario sighed and dropped his head back before wiping his hands down his face. "I'm not a killer," he whispered. "That ain't me."

Devonte frowned. "So you want to stay up under my grandmother forever?" he paused. "The deal was you take care of this hit and I'll put you and your girl up in a nice spot. And let me tell you something, with a bad bitch you got to have money to take care of her." Devonte paused. "It sounds like you scared to push off." His breath was heavy. "You asked for God's help and now it's time to step up."

Mario glanced over at Lauren and back at him. "Why you doing this to me? I've seen the people who work for you...you could get anybody." For some reason, and he couldn't explain, he felt Devonte was trying to put him into situations that would push him away from Lauren.

"Get your heart ready," Devonte responded. "Your debt is unpaid. It's time to settle."

"What's his name?" Mario frowned jaw twitching.

"Asher," Devonte replied menacingly.

Mario looked as if the wind had been pushed out of his belly. "Did you say Ash...Asher?"

"Yes..."

"Hector Asher Hernandez?" Mario said in a voice so low it resembled a whisper.

"Yes," Devonte said flatly.

"That's my cousin, man. I can't do that!"

"You can and you will. I want him to be haunted in his final hour. What better way than to be killed by his own blood?" he paused. "You and I both know this is why you were never able to live your life in freedom. Knowing that you walked away from the gang means he will never let you rest. Kill that nigga. Do it for yourself and your debt. Otherwise I'll kill you and that bitch myself... with my bare hands."

CHAPTER FIVE

Hustler Feud

A cool breeze tickled the leaves in the park where Stanford and Asher met. Ninny stood about twelve feet away with her back toward them... providing cover.

"Thanks for meeting me, man," Asher said, his body language screamed desperation. "I thought you were gonna leave me on my own with this dude."

Stanford clutched his hands behind him. "You've thanked me enough. Now tell me what's been going on."

"So God has the—"

"Call him by the name his mama gave him," Stanford said cutting him off with a wave of his hand. "He's no God of mine."

Asher nodded. "You right," he said softly before taking a moment to examine Stanford's tense stance. "Hold up...do you know him?" Stanford seemed highly emotional about a situation that he claimed he could care less about.

"Does it make a difference?"

Asher cleared his throat and decided to get to the point. "He's been wanting my blocks for awhile now. Truthfully he doesn't even need them. He owns half of Baltimore and makes money regardless of what I do."

"Tell me something...how do you run a business if you can't protect it? Even blue collars have insurance."

"My men are afraid of him," Asher said shamefully. "When I was in the gang things were cool. Stuff like this would never happen. But after they got arrested some time back, the soldiers went into prison. So I'm on my own right now with a few block monkeys who are too weak to be loyal."

"So why do you think he's doing this to you? I mean you claim he doesn't need the blocks...so why the grudge?"

"God," Asher cleared his throat recognizing his error. "I mean Devonte use to date my wife. When we broke up she became a part of the Harrington family. I missed her and after a lot of convincing she came back to me. Devonte resented me after that and six months after our breakup we were back together." Asher looked at him seriously. "You should know something very important. He hates to lose and can get violent if things don't go his way."

Stanford thought about the rape at Dove's. He was well aware of Devonte's behavior when he felt ousted but would not let that sway his interactions. "Give me a few days," Stanford said. "I'll see what I can do."

Stanford pulled up in a black Honda rental while the sky was dark purple and calling the vilest of characters to the streets. Four niggas dressed in dope boy clothing—oversized jeans and large t-shirts, had a pack of the purest dope in each pocket as they serviced the customers. They were Devonte's men, who arrested the block a few hours ago leaving Asher with no real estate.

Not believing in rushing things, Stanford sat quietly in the car observing their every move. He examined their body mechanics, like he did an opponent before stepping into the ring. When he was sure he had enough information, he turned his head. Giving Ninny a nod, she eased out of her tight blue jeans and jacket.

Sitting in her seat wearing only blue boy shorts and a white t-shirt, she stepped out of the car and walked the twenty so feet necessary to see the men. When the dealers saw her body and her albino features, they were intrigued and wondered since she was different, if her pussy was wetter than the average chick's too.

When she started moving her body in suggestive manners, they were in awe at how her hips swayed like the pendulum on a clock before going back and forth like a seesaw.

Dipping into their pockets, they pulled out dollar bills, never once thinking that the scenario didn't make any sense. After all, what was the cutie doing out after dark? With no clothes on?

It was too late for hypothesis, because while their dollars fell from the grasps onto her body, Stanford stepped out of the car, walked up the street and imprinted three times into the back of their skulls with a bullet.

When he kicked the bodies to the side, he saw that he turned his blonde haired beauty into a red head with their blood.

CHAPTER SIX

Only The Hardest

Mario sat in his ride, while looking at his cousin helping a baby out of the car seat in the front of a building. He was a fourteen month old with a wide smile and grabby hands, which needed hugs from his father every five minutes.

In the passenger seat was a black girl, with a big ass, cute face and skin darker than the outside layer of a coconut.

As he viewed his cousin, he wandered how was he able to switch from gang leader to a family man so quickly. Although Mario went legit, he always felt stifled because he never knew when Asher would reemerge from the darkness, stealing his happiness. "I don't want to kill you," he said to himself, hiding within his car. "Please give me a reason not too."

When Asher disappeared into the house, Mario took a fist to his face. Needing to feel more pain he struck himself in the left eye multiple times before moving from his lips to his cheek. His flesh opened under the pressure of his blows and when he looked at himself in the rear view mirror he looked like he did when he was first jumped into the Los Esqueletos. Except this time he did the blows to himself.

"I don't think I can do this," he said out loud. "I just can't."

Devonte walked into his grandmother's house while the Triad remained outside. "What are you doing here?" Lauren asked in the voice that drove him crazy. "Checking up on me?"

He smiled and closed the door behind himself. "Where is my grandmother?"

She looked at her clothes to make sure she didn't look to badly. "There was something going on at the church." She crossed her legs. "Why?"

He clicked his tongue a few times and walked to the couch before sitting down. "Does it matter?"

She rolled her eyes and he could feel the tension coming off of her body. "Why are you doing this? For me? And for Mario?"

He cocked his head to the right. "If someone brings you roses does it matter where they were pulled? Before God helped you were on your own. Now you have my assistance. Be grateful."

"I don't trust you," she said plainly. "I don't trust what you represent."

"Tell me, green eyes, what do you think I represent?"

"Evil," she said confidently.

He laughed. "You know what I think? I think you are a dope nigga's wife. And I think you try to hide from that because you were taught it was wrong, even though what you want is the best life has to offer a woman like you."

Her heart beat rapidly upon hearing what could be the truth she tried to deny. "Fuck are you talking about? I never gave you any information about me?"

She uncrossed her legs. "Men like you try to categorize everyone...well I can't be put into a box."

"You don't have to give me any info on you. Look how defensive you getting?" he continued calmly. "Your heart wants to be with a nigga like me but you can't allow yourself the pleasure. Because you feel it's wrong. But what you don't realize is once a dope nigga's wife always a dope nigga's wife and there's nothing you can do about it."

"That's where you got me wrong," she said trying to convince herself more than him. "I'm going to college for equine studies...and in case you don't know what it is it's the study of—"

"Horses," Devonte responded. When he sensed the surprise in her energy he said, "Don't be shocked, I'm not a dumb nigga. God knows all. But what I want you to also know is this...you can't buy horses by dealing with average Joes. Even the college studies you've chosen as a career means you have to have money to make it work."

"I can work for someone else," she said raising her chin.

"You sound stupid," he chuckled. "I mean let's be real, you won't work for someone else for the rest of your life."

"When I'm ready I'll get a job and buy my own," she shrugged.

"With what money? A thoroughbred horse costs about ten thousand dollars, and with training, equipment and vet visits you'll need about fourteen to twenty thousand a year. Who but a dope man can supply your need?"

Lauren was so angry, she was trembling. "You don't know me."

Devonte stood up and moved toward the door. "You will never be with Mario and it isn't because he doesn't want you. It's because he's too weak. In time you'll see." He walked out of the door and leaving her to her thoughts.

The twelve o'clock breeze on the roof of the building Devonte lived in was just right. He was having a meeting with the inner circle Harrington Family and Mario was invited.

"We lost three men on Asher's blocks the other day," Devonte said as he sipped from a glass of whiskey. "I know Asher is not smart enough to carry out his threat alone, so I figured he must've called in for reinforcements. After the men were killed the stash spot was raided leaving us with low product in that area. Now I never considered Asher a worthy adversary, but maybe I was wrong."

Not knowing what to say, Mario remained silent until he was spoken too.

"Does anybody know anything about this situation?" Devonte asked.

"We had eyes on Asher all that night," Tykisha said. "And he never left our sight. Whoever pushed off wasn't him."

"She's right, God," Samantha said.

"You're telling me what I already know."

"God, I know you don't want to consider this but I have to say it," Heather started. "Why don't we let Asher have the blocks? It wasn't until we got into a turf battle that we experienced any rift. By not handling the situation immediately, we expose ourselves to threats on the real estate we earned."

And They Call Me God

"Especially if people start thinking we're weak since we haven't fired back at our attackers," Samantha added.

"So we have a problem and the answer you bring me is to run?" Devonte said. The room went silent. "Leaving the blocks is not an option once we laid claim to them. The only thing we should be considering is what needs to happen to keep what we claimed. Nothing more nothing less."

When the doorbell rang Tykisha went to answer it. A few seconds later she returned with Varro who was fuming mad when he saw Mario. Looking down at him he said, "Wait...what is he doing here?"

Confused at what he was talking about Devonte asked, "What difference does it make who I invite to my table?"

Varro's nose flared. "So you're the reason I can't find her?" he asked Devonte. "You're the reason she was taken off the streets. And vanished into thin air."

Devonte contemplated what was said and exhaled. "So you're the one who hit her in the truck and ran?"

"No, I was the one protecting her," he lied.

"Tell the truth, nigga," Mario responded angrily. "You ran her over and left her to die. If I hadn't called the ambulance she wouldn't be alive."

"Devonte, if you got the girl give her to me," Varro said ignoring Mario. "Don't let this Spaniard come in between our business."

Now Devonte was interested. "Why would he come in between us? When you've been married to a bitch in California for ten years?" He paused. "Come on, man. You can't be tripping over no side chick."

Mario was flabbergasted upon hearing that Varro was married. He knew Lauren was unaware and would never have been with him if she knew.

Varro took a deep breath, looked down at Mario and then Devonte. He was tired of talking about Lauren when he came on more important matters. "You're right," he paused. "I'm just here to tell you that Asher came to me with some product that's packaged like yours. I know because we both buy from the Kennedy family and it's the same quality. What do you want me to do?"

"Why would he come to you when he knows you deal with God?" Tykisha asked suspiciously.

"Because he was desperate to make some cash. Who knows?"

As they conversed, although his mind should've been on business, Devonte considered Lauren. He wondered what made her so appealing that two men would fight over her. And more importantly should he enter the ring?

"Varro, we have it from here," Devonte said. "But stay by the phone, I'll tell you if that changes."

Before leaving Varro looked down at Mario once more and walked out.

Lauren called Mario several times to bring her something to eat. Although Aubrey had been an outstanding host, lately she'd been out with friends and buying new things for her new house Devonte purchased her. Leaving her by herself.

Originally she didn't mind staying in the house, due to fear of Varro finding her. But the curiosity for life got the best of her and she needed to spread her wings.

And They Call Me God

She grabbed one of her wooden crutches, hopped to the table and pulled out the fifty dollars from her purse before stuffing the money in her pocket. Since one of her legs was still in a cast as well as one of her arms, she needed the crutch to get around. She opened the door, locked the bottom lock and hopped outside. She knew Aubrey would be furious if her neighbors saw her but she needed fresh air.

The moment she turned the corner Samantha, Heather and Tykisha got out of a black Suburban and followed her on foot. At first she thought they were about to jump her until she recognized their faces from the hospital. "What do you want?" she asked rolling her eyes.

"We are here to protect you," Tykisha explained as they continued their walk. "So where we going?"

Lauren balanced herself on her crutch and turned to look at them. "Listen, I don't know who sent you…"

"Mario," Samantha said softly.

"First of all I know every person in Mario's life and he never knew you. So it must be Devonte."

"God," Heather said correcting her. "We call him God."

Irritated by all three of them, Lauren turned around and proceeded to walk. When she almost fell and Tykisha tried to help her, Lauren slapped her in the face so hard the corner of her right eye bled. Out of reflex Tykisha busted her in the face and when she went down, stomped her in the side of her cheek with her shoe cracking her face open slightly.

Lauren sat on the edge of a bed in the emergency room getting stitched up. Samantha, Heather and Tykisha sat in the hallway outside of Lauren's room waiting for Devonte. When they saw him coming down the hall, clicking his mouth with The Triad following they stood up.

"I'm so sorry, God," Tykisha said stepping in front of him. "She was trying to leave and we followed her and then…"

"You hit her," he said calmly.

"It wasn't like that," Samantha said. "She really tried to keep her distance but the girl swung on her first."

"Go home," Devonte said not feeling like arguing. "I'll talk to you later."

No one left right away but Samantha moved closer. "Are you mad at me?"

"If I were mad you would know."

"I love you, God," Samantha said, fearing she would be thrown out of the family.

"Go," he yelled.

Before Devonte walked into Lauren's room, Tykisha stepped closer. She had a question and contemplated not asking since Samantha just pissed him off. "God, have you given any more thought to what I asked? About my little girl living with us?"

"We'll talk about it later," he said through clenched teeth. "That's your problem. You never know the right time and place."

"I'm sorry, you're right," she said proceeding down the hall with her progeny.

Devonte walked into the room to see Lauren and Greco followed. Clicking his mouth a few times Devonte took a seat in a chair in the corner. "You can leave us alone," he said to Greco who quickly walked away. When he was gone he asked, "Are you okay?"

"Nice girls," she said holding her stitched up jaw.

"They were there for your protection...Mario requested it."

"You think I don't know that they were there because you sent them?" she explained. "I know everybody Mario has ever known. He doesn't have that kind of –"

"Power," he said finishing her sentence.

She was embarrassed to admit he was right so she sighed. "Listen, this is not our lifestyle. We are not these kind of people...and by we I mean me and Mario."

"Mario is free to leave whenever he wants," he said. "I'm not keeping him here and I'm not keeping you either." He paused. "Do you want me to tell the security to leave? Do you want me to tell my grandmother to put you out? And to cancel the work that Mario is doing for us that will earn you a little money on the side? Play God for a day and it will all go away."

Lauren thought about Varro and thought about how safe she felt under Devonte's camp. "I don't know what I want," she said softly.

"You're thinking too hard. Try and go with the flow. Trust me, things will be much better." Devonte stood up and moved toward the door. Before leaving out he said, "You're safe with me...I want you to know that."

He walked away.

Fifteen minutes later Lauren was lying on the bed preparing to go home. She was waiting on the bill to see how much damage the visit would cost her when an elderly white woman with purple grey hair walked inside and said, "You are free to go."

Sighing she asked, "How much is this going to cost me?"

"Nothing," she said looking over the paperwork. "Everything has been taking care of in cash by Devonte Harrington."

Lauren smiled but quickly wiped it away. She slid off of the bed and was about to find a ride back to Aubrey's when Chicago and Shaw walked inside the room and said, "You ready? We're here to take you home."

"How do you know I couldn't get there myself?"

"Once God watches over you, you don't have to worry about a thing," Shaw said with a smile. "We're ready when you are."

Lauren was sleeping heavily on Aubrey's sofa when she turned over to get comfortable. Her eyes opened for a moment and when they did she saw Mario leaning on the wall with a bruised face. She popped up and said, "Oh my god, what happened to you?"

He peeled himself off of the wall and moved toward her. Easing to his knees he grabbed her hands and looked into her eyes. "I love you, Lauren," he responded avoiding the question. "I always have." Pregnant puddles of sweat began to form around his hairline. "And I know this is coming at a weird time but I wanted you to know."

"Mario, you're scaring me," she said as she panted heavily. "You come in here with a banged up face, confessing your love."

"Don't be scared," he said as his eyes bulged, as if he'd been up for five days straight. "Just know that I've been holding that on my chest for a long time," he said softly. "I also want you to know that I'm about to make a serious decision for both of us. One that will mean you will never have to worry about the lifestyle you deserve again."

"But I don't care about none of that," she said.

He looked deeper into her eyes. "I see how you look at these females out here holding the latest bag and wearing the newest shoes."

She felt shallow as she considered her unconscious actions. "I don't...I don't know why I..."

He wiped his sweaty forehead. "Don't come down on yourself. You use to having it all and I get that, but I need you to be in agreement with what you really want. Otherwise you will never be happy."

"What do you want me to say, Mario?"

"Say that you want the best...and then let me do what I can to give it to you."

Her heart beat rapidly upon hearing his request. It was as if she was an addict and someone was holding the drug of her choice right before her face. "I...I want..."

"Say it," he said gripping her hands tighter.

She took a deep breath, swallowed and looked into his eyes. "I want the good life," she said softly. And then more confidently she said, "I want it all."

"Well I'm going to give it to you and it won't be via the lifestyle you want but I will never involve your safety or your freedom." He paused. "Do you trust me?"

She nodded. "But I don't want you hurt, Mario. If having the good life means you will be harmed than it's not important to me."

His stomach bubbled and his heart kicked up speed. Not only had she proven he'd chosen the right woman, but she validated his feelings by caring about his safety. "I'll be okay. I just want to know that it won't be for nothing."

Something told her to tell him no, and to keep their friendship in tact, but she cared about him although it wasn't love. Mario had always been in the picture and when he connected with Devonte he had done a lot to keep her safe. Already he was harder than she could've imagined and for that he deserved a little respect.

"Yes," she whispered. "Yes I will be with you."

They kissed passionately, before holding each other tightly.

✝

Asher walked into the house and removed his shoes at the front door of his apartment. Exhausted from making moves all day, he dropped his jeans, and t-shirt on a trail toward the bathroom. He figured he'd take a shower, grab a quick nap and visit his baby mother later so he could see his daughter.

Once inside the bathroom, he was shocked when he saw Mario sitting on the toilet aiming a .45 in his direction. For a second he tried to pretend he was happy to see his blood relative but his terror was obvious by the way his breath burst from his body in short quick spurts.

"Primo, I didn't—"

"Don't say anything," Mario said softly. "Don't tell me that you're happy to see me. Or that you love me. It won't do any good."

Asher leaned up against the wall and sighed. "Then what the fuck you doing here?"

Mario stood up and said, "I came to put you out of your misery so that I can have my freedom."

"Are you sure that's the real reason you're going to kill me?" Asher asked. "Or do you have another accomplice who's pulling strings?"

"Even if I did does it matter?" he paused. "After I left the Los Esqueletos I didn't have freedom. At one point I got use to it and even grew comfortable always having to look over my shoulders. But now I have someone I love and she deserves better."

Asher nodded. "God sent you...right?"

"Yes...but it's still my work."

Asher shook his head. "Don't you understand why he's doing this? It's over my first wife, primo. He wanted her and when she left him for me he never got over it. I don't know who fucked up his mind but he has a thing about women. And if you have one he wants you will never be safe."

Hearing what resembled the truth about his current circumstance made him uncomfortable. "It may or may not be true...but right now I need peace."

"And you get that by killing me?"

"That's the plan," he responded.

"It's not necessary, Mario. The gang is dismantled. Don't be stupid."

When Mario looked down for a second, Asher pushed him toward the sofa and ran toward the front door. While he darted away, Mario fired at him but the gum jammed. When he saw the gleam of a knife's blade in the kitchen he dipped toward it, snatched it out of the block just before Asher grabbed his gun that was sitting on the living room table.

Mario knocked him to the floor, crawled on top of his body and stabbed him multiple times in the

By T. Styles   131

stomach and the face. The sound of bone crushing under each thrash reminded him about how much damage he was doing. Asher had given up fighting a long time ago but for a final act of vengeance, Mario raised the knife and brought it across his throat.

When Asher's eyes rolled to the back of his head and the breath crawled from his body, Mario squirmed a few feet from him and vomited all over his clothing.

Devonte stood on the balcony and inhaled the night air that blew over the inner harbor. Needing to talk to him, Greco opened the sliding door and said, "He's here."

Devonte nodded. "Let him in."

Mario walked outside and placed his clammy hands on the balcony. He was still covered in his cousin's dried blood. "It's done," he said trembling. "You have something too..."

"Samantha," Devonte yelled as his gaze remained outward over the dark sparkling water. Devonte knew what he was about to ask before the words exited his lips.

She came quickly with two glasses of whiskey and a full bottle. She handed Devonte one and Mario the other. "I hope you like my liquor of choice," Devonte said to him.

Mario answered by downing it, handing it back saying, "Another please."

She quickly fulfilled his request five more times and Devonte patiently waited until Mario got the necessary buzz. When he sensed he had enough he said, "You have something to tell me?"

"It's done," Mario repeated. "He's gone."

Devonte nodded. "How do you feel?"

"Like shit," he sobbed heavily and his soul felt like it was pulling from his body. "I...I can't breathe...I can't."

"Pull yourself together," Devonte said unsympathetically. "You already did the deed...now it's time to enjoy the fruit of your labor."

Silence.

Mario took a deep breath, exhaled and stood straight. "I will never forget or forgive you for what you did to me. But that won't impact my loyalty for you giving me the woman of my dreams."

Devonte adjusted the GOD medallion around his neck— placing it in the center of his chest. "Then I guess it was all worth it." His arms fell by his sides. "Go home. And if she lets you, fuck you're bitch."

Mario nodded and walked away.

When he left Greco walked outside. "God, you know I don't question your authority, but what is your thing with Mario and Lauren? I don't trust it for us." He paused. "Besides, look at how he talks to you."

Devonte laughed knowing that Greco meant well. "You have dogs right?"

"Yes."

"When they growl a few times do you love them any less?"

"No, God."

"Well I don't like animals...but I find Mario and Lauren intriguing. At the same time, if he bites, I have no problem snapping his neck."

Devonte, Heather, Tykisha and Samantha were sitting at Morgan's Steakhouse eating expensive meals and drinking liquor. The Triad sat at a table next to them and they were wasted. Asher being dead meant the Harrington family was victorious.

They were on their third bottle of wine and having a good time when Tykisha decided to get serious. "Devonte," she said softly. "I really need to talk to you about my little girl."

Devonte exhaled because every other day she was coming at him with the same shit. Originally he was going to tell her that there would be no chance but for some reason he didn't. Maybe part of him liked that she begged.

"What is it, Tykisha?" he said coldly, the others angry that she was ruining the day. "We're celebrating. Why you coming at me about this shit now?"

"She is about to be placed up for adoption," she said doing her best not to make him angrier. "But God, she's a good little girl. She's seven years old and reading on a ninth grade level."

His nose flared. "When you first were accepted into this family I told you that there could only be God. You said you understood, got on your knees and accepted, forsaking all others."

"And I still want this," she said wide-eyed. "More than anything."

"Are you sure about that?" he asked through clenched teeth. "Because your actions are showing me differently."

Her heart pumped harder. "God, I don't want to lose her into the system. If she's adopted out then I will never see her again." She paused as she felt tears pushing out of her eyes. "I can't be without her any longer."

"Then it sounds like you've made your choice," he snapped his fingers. "Chicago, get her out of my space...I can't breathe."

At first Chicago looked confused, because he fucked with Tykisha. In the family the two of them were the closest. But Devonte gave an order and the last thing you did was disobey a command. So he stood up and grabbed Tykisha by the arm.

"Before you escort her out take my clothes off of her first," he responded.

"God, please don't do this," Tykisha said looking at everyone staring in her direction.

Samantha and Heather pressed their hands over their mouths. Seeing her like that broke their hearts but she knew the rules just like they all did. Upsetting Devonte meant the penalty was isolation.

When Tykisha saw the pain in Chicago's face for being forced to handle her roughly, she slowly removed her clothes while shooting rays of hate in Devonte's direction. She didn't want Chicago to do his dirty work. His eyes were covered with his signature dark shades so she couldn't see them. But she knew he was aware of how badly he was hurting her. Although tears rolled down her face she was determined not to give him anymore.

The scene stunned the patrons but the manager's didn't stop the matter. Besides, Devonte spent enough money in the steakhouse to pay for the lease for six months.

In a public restaurant she stripped out of her jeans, blouse and shoes. Standing before him in her red bra set she said, "I still love you. But I love my daughter too."

"Then go be with that bitch," he said.

She walked toward the exit leaving the family.

There was fifteen minutes of cold silence until Devonte said, "If you aren't with me you're against me." He paused. "Anybody else have anything to say about the matter?"

"No," everyone said one by one.

"Then let's enjoy the rest of the," Devonte's sentence was severed when bullets crashed into the windows. Glass shattered everywhere causing the Harrington family to fall to the floor for protection. Patrons screaming in the background made the tension in the air higher.

Who was trying to attack?

Greco yanked Devonte down and pushed him under the table for cover. The girls followed...all but one.

"Where the fuck is Heather?" Greco asked. When he saw her arm dangling, he pulled her down. Her eyes were wide opened and the bloodied dot on her forehead that resembled a bindi told them all what happened.

She was murdered.

Devonte stood on his balcony covered in Heather's dried blood. The Triad posted on the walls around him.

And They Call Me God

"Who the fuck tried to kill me?" he roared. "Who would be crazy enough to take an aim at me when they know what I'm capable of?"

The Triad remained silent although they had a few ideas.

"So nobody has anything to say?" he yelled again.

"God, what about the new kid," Greco asked trying not to appear too lax at his line of questioning. "You said yourself he was shook up about the job you had him carry out. Maybe he wanted to get even."

Devonte considered the question but he didn't like him for the murder attempt. "It doesn't feel like him." he paused. "If he wanted to kill me he had a chance when he came to my house the other day after it was done."

Chicago and Shaw looked at each other believing he was too blind when it came to his new project. "What about Varro?" Shaw said. "He seemed mad he couldn't get his way with the girl."

Devonte nodded. "Keep eyes on him for the next few weeks. Don't let him out of your sight. When I get enough information I'll tell you the next move."

After the first hit on Devonte's family, with many more planned, Ninny was lying face down on the bed in their hotel room while Stanford ran his hard wet tongue down the crack of her ass.

It was celebration time.

Stanford wasn't trying to kill Devonte at the shootout earlier. Besides, he had him in his sights and would've been successful if he wanted. The plan was to take the things he loved, like he did him at Dove's School For Boys.

Stanford penetrated her hole delving deeper, causing her pussy to moisten even more. It was pointy-wet and hard the way she liked it.

Easing her fingers under her pelvis, she flipped her clit off to the sensation of his strokes, before exploding on her fingertips. Turning over and said, "I want you to fuck my face."

He winked at her, loving her nasty ways. "I aim to please," he responded as he crawled on the bed and over her mouth. Stanford grabbed her by the back of the head, squatted over her face and poked his long dick down her throat. She sucked, slurped and squeezed his thickness with her jaws until she felt him pulsating.

As he felt the softness of her mouth he couldn't last a minute longer before he exploded into her throat.

When he was done he crawled next to her and said, "You ready to finish this nigga off?"

She nodded. "Whatever you want to do I'm with," she said before they kissed sloppily and fucked all over again.

CHAPTER SEVEN

Time Doesn't Heal All

MONTHS LATER

Samantha and The Triad brought boxes into Devonte's grandmother's new house in New Carrolton, Maryland, as Devonte sat in the living room on the sofa. The three-bedroom home was just the right size and she was beside herself with joy. When the last boxes were brought in, The Triad placed up her new curtains trying to get her crib together.

Over the months Devonte, Lauren and Mario's relationship grew weirder to all those around. For starters they would spend a lot of time over Aubrey's and when they weren't with her they would go to the movies, dinner and even many vacations together. It was as if Lauren had two boyfriends and certain members of the Harrington family were starting to get jealous of the grown dynamic.

Aubrey walked up to Devonte and sat next to him. "I can't believe you did this for me."

He laughed. "Why? Because you don't deserve it?"

She laughed. "You're still hurting over that white girl getting killed aren't you?" she paused. "And now you want to take it out on me."

"You don't know what you talking about," he said as he adjusted his shades.

"I know enough to realize that being mad at other people won't bring her back. Aubrey looked around the living room again and said, "I can't believe this is all mine. And that my grandson gave it to me."

He smiled and she grabbed his hand. "Come with me. I want you to see something right quick."

He stood up and she walked him to the back of the house, in the kitchen. When they made it to a sliding door she pushed it to the right revealing a large backyard. "Because of you I can grow my own vegetables now." She hugged him again and looked up at him. "All organics from now on." She said excitedly. "Now I have something I want to give to you."

Devonte clicked his mouth a few times and walked over to the kitchen table...she followed. "You don't have to do anything for me." He sat down and readjusted the cross on his chest. "I can buy anything I desire."

"Except this," she replied. She strolled over to a red ceramic cookie jar on the counter shaped like a heart, picked up the top and looked inside. Aubrey removed a small piece of paper, advanced toward him and placed it in his hand. "It's yours."

He took it from her. "What is this?"

"Your father's address."

"Why you giving this to me now?" he paused. Months ago he wanted it but now he wasn't interested. "You aren't afraid I would still kill this nigga?"

She sighed and sat next to him. "Because the lifestyle you're leading will soon lead to death. And before you die I want you to make right with those who you can't forgive."

He felt gut punched. "Why would you say some shit like that to me?" he yelled. "Fuck wrong with you? I bought you this house and that's how you come at me?"

And They Call Me God

"You are living foul, Devonte. You don't think I know how you getting this money? Having folks running around here calling you God?" she said waving him off. "You have a darkness surrounding you that you had since you were a child. I finally understand it but before you leave here I want you to make peace."

He slammed the paper on the table. "I'm not interested in him or Angela."

She opened and closed her mouth as the right words left her. "Son—"

"Grandma, I don't care about dude no more. Do you know the only thing he ever gave me? A pair of Jordan's. And the only reason he did that was to get in my mother's pussy." His posture was rigid. "He wasn't interested in me so why should I be interested in him. Tell him to fuck off."

"He doesn't know I'm telling you."

Devonte's eyes widened and then he laughed. "So you want me to go begging for daddy back?" he asked sarcastically. "Come on, grams. I'm a grown man. I don't need daddy no more."

Aubrey looked lovingly at her grandson. She walked over to the table, picked up the address and tucked it in his front jean pocket. "I'm not sure, but I think he's changed now. He's a preacher at a church and if you knew what kind of lifestyle your father led you would be surprised." She paused. "Go introduce yourself and see what happens."

"This shit is crazy," he said shaking his head. "I'm not doing that shit."

"What have you ever done unselfishly? With no strings attached? I mean have you ever loved another without expecting anything in return? In life, love is the only thing that sets us free."

By T. Styles   141

Samantha walked into the kitchen, her bare feet scratching against the floor. "God, is there anything else I can do for you?" She asked wide-eyed.

"Not now, Sam," he said still irritated with Aubrey.

She smiled at his grandmother and Devonte before walking away.

"That child is touched," she said under her breath.

"Aren't we all?"

"God, Mario and Lauren are here," Chicago said entering the kitchen. "They said they have good news."

"Tell them to come back," he said standing up.

Mario and Lauren walked into the kitchen holding hands. While Lauren's top lip was tucked into her mouth, Mario was so excited he couldn't keep still. Throughout the weeks he had grown close to Aubrey and even began to see Devonte a little differently. He could never forgive him for what he made him do to Asher, but he realized in order for him to lead his life it had to be done.

"What's up?" Devonte said, sensing Lauren's uncomfortable energy.

"We're getting married," he said excitedly. "I asked and she said yes."

Aubrey slapped her hands against her face and then hugged Mario tightly, while Devonte and Lauren stood quietly in the same space.

PRESENT DAY

The interview was longer than Samantha thought it would be as she sat in her seat and sighed. "I was there during the announcement of the marriage," Samantha sighed. "In his grandmother's house playing the background as usual. But instead of Devonte being angry over losing Lauren to the marriage proposal, I saw something different. It was like...well it was like he was turning over a new leaf. Had come to terms with letting her go."

"New leaf?" June asked.

"Don't get me wrong, I know he loved Lauren," she paused. "Because of how he talked about her." She sighed. "I wanted him to think about me the same way."

"Did you tell him?"

"No," she paused. "You don't tell God who to love. He picks who he picks and if you're lucky you're the one."

Heidi exhaled. "What was Mario and Devonte's relationship like after the proposal?"

Samantha gazed into the room. "Do you like video games?" she asked.

Both detectives shook their heads no, and tried to hide their irritation. They didn't feel much like analogies and wanted to stick to the facts.

"Well, I'm a big fan of a game called Fantasy Beauties," she said. "And in the game you pick the person you want to be—hair, clothes, career and even mate. The unique thing is, within the game you get to meet other people who are also choosing to live their lives through avatars."

By T. Styles   143

"You're losing me," June said.

"What I'm trying to say is I think Devonte fell back on his quest to get Lauren because he got to puppet the relationship through Mario." She crossed her legs. "Mario may have thought he was in control but he was nothing more than a placemat. And I'm not sure but I believe unconsciously both Devonte and Lauren were aware of it."

Debra Wallows, another detective, opened the door. "Detectives, I have a message for you."

"Excuse us for a second," June said as they stepped out into the hallway.

"What's up?" Heidi asked.

"He's on his way," she said. "You may want to hurry her along."

"We haven't gotten to the massacre yet," June responded.

Debra shrugged. "If I were you I'd make it quick. The one this is all about is on the way. Why delay?"

June and Heidi looked at one another and walked back through the door with hopes to bring Samantha's testimony to an end.

When they were back inside Samantha said, "I have to tell you something...just because he turned over a new leaf as far as Lauren was concerned, didn't mean the rest of us didn't suffer."

PART THREE

CHAPTER EIGHT

Drunk Dreams

Lauren straddled Mario as he stroked in and out of her body on their ten thousand dollar custom-made bed. A month ago they moved into a beautiful loft in downtown Baltimore, not too far from Devonte's and for a while Lauren felt on top of the world.

But she was realizing money wasn't everything because something in Mario changed. He seemed possessed by inner demons she never knew about.

While they continued to enjoy each other's bodies, she looked deeply into his eyes, trying to connect with that something she felt a few months ago when he first asked her to be his wife. But as hard as she tried the association wasn't there anymore. Something happened to him that he wouldn't share with her, and as a result the friendship was suffering as well as their pending engagement.

"I love you, Lauren," he said before kissing her deeply. "I always have...please don't leave me."

Struck by his pleading words she stopped moving, got up and lie on her side of the bed. His penis, still damp with her juice, was deflating. "Where did that come from?" she asked. "Mario, I don't know about us anymore," she exhaled.

"What did I do?"

"Every time we make love you ask me not to leave you. It's like you're trying to ask for forgiveness for something I don't know about." She rolled over so that she could face him and he positioned himself so that he could look into her eyes.

"I don't know what it is," he lied. What really bothered him was that he'd killed his cousin and he couldn't get it out of his heart or mind. "You're distant," he said misplacing the energy. "And the strongest connection you have with someone isn't with me."

She eased out of bed. "Not this shit again."

"It's fucking true," he said loudly. "You don't think I see you and Devonte's friendship growing stronger than our relationship?"

"You're making things up. If anything since we said we were getting married he left us be. He doesn't even hang out with us that much anymore."

"So you an expert on him now?"

"Fuck this shit," she said as she attempted to get out of bed. But he stopped her movements by wrapping his hand around her throat and squeezing. She scratched at his hands until he finally released.

Immediately remorseful he said, "I'm sorry, baby. I'm so — "

"Fuck you!" she yelled. "I'm sick of this shit. You've been drinking non-stop lately and you act like...you act like you don't deserve to have me. If that's how you feel then let me go...but please stop taking your insecurities out on me like a bitch!" She ran to the bathroom.

Still focused on the closed bathroom door, when the phone rang Mario reluctantly answered. "Hello."

"Damn, Mario, I figured you'd be a little more happy to hear from me!" Devonte yelled.

Mario laughed. "I know, God!" he joked. "We were just getting ready for the club."

"Well hurry up. The limo will be by your house in an hour! I'm riding with ya'll and meeting the family down there."

"I'll be ready," Mario responded looking at the door.

When he ended the call he walked over to the dresser, grabbed the bottle of vodka and poured half down his throat. When he put it down Lauren was standing behind him, gazing at him through squinted eyes. "I can't keep doing this, Mario. You gonna have to push back on the liquor or we're through."

"I know baby," he said with a half smile. "Just give me a few days...I'll get my shit together. I promise."

Lauren walked back into the bathroom and looked at herself in the mirror. Her face was thinner than normal because she was so stressed. She ran her hand over her gaunt jaws, and she opened her mouth wide and screamed in silence.

Devonte and Mario were sitting in the back of the limo smoking a blunt. Devonte didn't do other drugs but the weed he never passed up. When they were done, they pressed it out in the ashtray and rolled down the window to allow the smoke to escape.

Lauren sat on the right side of the limo looking at them. Across from them were more glasses and a mirror. Although she would normally participate tonight was different...she wasn't in the mood. Devonte grabbed the bottle of whiskey to his right, poured himself a glass before handing Mario both glasses to give one to Lauren.

"I'm not feeling like drinking," she said softly. "But you two can have fun."

"Come on, baby," Mario pleaded. He got up from his seat and sat on the right side of her. "I thought you said you would try to have a good time before we left the house. What changed?"

She looked at him closely, reminding him that he should be aware of why she was unhappy. After all, not even an hour ago he was choking her out. "Like I said, I just don't feel like drinking."

Devonte, realizing his birthday party was about to go to shit, got up and sat on the other side of her. "Not even for my birthday?" he asked pushing his dark shades closer to his face.

She smiled a little and Mario noticed immediately how happier she appeared since Devonte was closer. "Hand me the drink, Mario," Devonte said.

He obeyed.

"Let's put the drama to the side for one night," he held the drink out and she took it from his hand. "Thanks, sis."

Upon witnessing the ultimate betrayal on her part, Mario felt like caving her face in from one side to the other. He tried to hide his jealousy but whatever Devonte had over her was too hard to deny. He started to question his manliness. Maybe he wasn't as hard as Devonte. Maybe if he reacted more violently she would look at him like she looked at Devonte.

Once again Devonte's charm won her over and it was evident by the drink she was holding in her hand that she claimed she didn't want. "To God, and to you both," he smiled. "May you be happy forever, only separating by death."

The club was packed as Devonte, Lauren and Mario walked onto the scene. Tiny soft light bulbs were embedded into the black ceiling making it look like they were under the stars. The Triad fell in line behind the trio as they walked deeper inside. And the moment the DJ caught the sparkle of Devonte's gold chain with a diamond studded cross he took to the mic.

"Ladies and gentlemen its what you've all been waiting for. God has blessed us with his presence. Now you know what that means! He needs ten of the baddest bitches to rush to the VIP for approval and from what I see tonight the competition is thick! Have fun ladies."

Mario shook his head as women made a beeline for the VIP section all to get up under Devonte. Drunk and angry at Laurens' dismissal of his feelings, he hung over God's shoulder as if he was his closest comrade. You my hero," Mario yelled acting like a coat clown. "I fucking love you, man!"

Greco pressed him a little. "Ease up, man."

Samantha grabbed Devonte's hand, taking him away from Mario and Lauren and whisking him toward the VIP. Lauren saw the gold diggers surrounding them and she didn't approve. Why did she care about him so much? For the life of her she couldn't understand. There seemed to be something powerful and powerless about him at the same time but she couldn't put her finger on what.

Could it be their pasts? Both volatile and both unstable, that made their quiet connection so strong?

And They Call Me God

The last thing she wanted was to destroy the new relationship the three of them seemed to have so she put her personal feelings aside. But it did nothing for her jealousy.

"I'm going over to VIP," Devonte announced to Mario and Lauren. "Ya'll coming?" Samantha maintained the hold she had on Devonte's hand as if he were fragile.

"No, I wouldn't want to shit on your parade," Lauren said a little more enviously than she realized. "Plus we have our own. We'll be across the way."

Devonte kissed Lauren on the cheek, causing electric shocks to shoot through her body. He gave Mario some dap and said, "See you in a minute."

"Do you," Mario said with a grin on his face that felt more like a frown inside. When Devonte left, he took a moment to glance at his fiancé who was smiling a little too much. "You know as hard as you try that he'll never want you right?"

Lauren, surprised at his comment, blinked a few times. "What are you talking about?"

"I'm not blind, Lauren," he yelled when the music seemed to get louder. "I see how you look at him. And even in the limo ride over here. I've seen it from the first moment we met. I just hoped it would go away."

"Stop trying to start a fight and be a man," she said as she stomped toward their VIP table.

✝

Devonte sat back in the plush black sofa as The Triad decided which women was worthy enough to be in VIP. When the limit had been reached they shoed everyone else away until a cutie wearing a tight black dress with ankle strapped sandals stepped up.

"We good on the bitches," Chicago said with a shove to the woman's face without even looking at her closely. "Be gone."

She stumbled backwards until she stood up and said, "Chicago, it's me. Tykisha!"

The moment Devonte heard her voice over the music he said, "Let that bitch in!"

She clutched her purse close to her body and then relaxed a little. Everyone from The Triad smiled and even Samantha was happy to see her. Nervously, Tykisha sat next to him. "Hey, God."

Silence.

"I know you told me to go away, but I couldn't," she continued. "And I heard what happened to Heather. I wanted to tell you and the family I was sorry and was hoping that you'd take me back." She paused. "I was a fool. Losing Heather made me realize how dumb it was to leave. Without the family I don't have shit."

"That's why you wanted in VIP?" he asked adjusting his medallion so that the diamonds would be right side up. "To tell me something I already know?"

She adjusted uneasily in her seat. "What I got to do for you to accept me back? I'm willing to do anything."

Devonte leaned against the brick wall in the alley of the club while Tykisha was on her knees sucking his dick. He could've used one of the Private rooms inside, or even took her to his place, but he wanted to treat her as slutty as possible, to showcase to her how it felt to fall from grace. Right before he came he snatched his dick from her mouth and busted all over her face. Afterwards he pissed on her and to his surprise she took it all.

Tucking his dick back into his pants he said, "How does it feel? To lose my love?"

"I just want to be back with you, God. I don't have nowhere else I want to be. My daughter is with a family who loves her and I need to be back with mine."

He didn't seem receptive so she went harder.

"Please," she pleaded. "Give me a chance and you'll never hear me choose anything or anybody over you ever again. I promise."

Devonte looked down at her, laughed and knocked on the door to his right. When it opened she was left on her knees.

Defeated and embarrassed, she fell down and cried heavily into her palms. She was about to stand up and take the walk of shame, when the door opened again and Chicago tossed a bucked of ice water on her face before opening a few bottles of water and doing the same.

"What was that for?" she asked frowning at him.

"God told me to baptize you and then take you back to the crib." He scratched his head. "Whatever that shit was that caused you to be out of the family, don't do it again. Okay? You saved now. When one person in the family fucks up its bad news for everybody."

He helped her up as she grinned all the way to the car.

✝

On the way back to the party, Devonte and Greco ran into Lauren who was coming from the bathroom. *U Remind Me* by R. Kelly was playing as she walked up to them. "Can I talk to Devonte in private?" she asked.

"Who?" Greco frowned.

She cleared her throat. "I mean God."

Greco looked at Devonte who nodded and walked away.

When they were alone Lauren grabbed his hand.

"Why you want the privacy? You want to dance or something?"

She tried to hide her smile and act uninterested but it was hard when it came to Devonte. "Get out of here, boy."

Instead of leaving she allowed him to be more playfully aggressive with her until she was in his arms, her breasts pressed against his chest. He was drunk with liquor and power but when it came to Lauren his feelings were real.

So they danced.

Until the song was over.

Knowing all the while that they shouldn't be touching one another.

She looked up at him. "Why do you always wear shades?"

"Take them off," he said. "I don't mind you looking in my eyes."

She did and his eyes looked as if they held a lot of pain. Maybe that *something* that was bothering him was the reason she gravitated toward him.

Placing the shades back on he separated from her. "I don't know what's going on with you and Mario but things are going to be okay. He loves you."

Her lips separated slightly before closing again. She wanted to tell him that the last thing she was thinking about was Mario but would it be disloyal? Instead she kissed him on the cheek and said, "Happy Birthday, Devonte. Thank you for coming in our lives when we needed you most."

She walked away, disappearing into the bright lights of the club.

Devonte, Mario and The Triad sat in their boardroom going over the issue of the day—one of their stash spots had been hit. "How the fuck did this happen?" Devonte yelled. "Asher is not around anymore. And I thought we had eight men on those blocks at all times?"

"The cops came past the spot at one time," Greco said since he was in charge of the men. "They couldn't go back on the block until the heat died down which it didn't for a long time. By the time they did someone had already hit us."

"The cops?" Devonte said. "We have five-o on salary. They would've let us known if something was coming down."

"That's what I'm not understanding either," Greco responded.

Devonte sat back, his head moving from left to right. He adjusted his shades and said, "Whoever rolled up on the block wasn't cops." Devonte wrecked his mind trying to identify who would be so stupid.

He stood up and paced in place.

"We need a new stash house," he continued. "Somewhere off the grid that won't be suspected." He addressed all of his men. "Work on it and don't come back until you have an answer."

Devonte and Mario were at a small bar in Baltimore City throwing back shots of whiskey. The Triad, although not directly behind Devonte, remained close. "What's up with you and Lauren?" Devonte asked Mario. "Every time I turn around ya'll are beefing."

Mario sighed. "From the day you first helped us, your fascination with her has never waivered. Why?"

He laughed. "You know you're the only one who I allow to talk to me like that. And yet if you ever did it in front of the family I would kill you."

Mario smiled although he knew he was serious.

"I respect your relationship with Lauren," Devonte replied. "Understand if I didn't you would know by now."

Mario twisted the watch on his arm before stopping. "I don't know what's up with her." He sipped his drink. "But I'm tired of trying to figure it out." Mario scratched his elbow. "Sometimes I'd rather be single."

"So is the wedding still on?"

"As far as I know, but for real if you want the answer you have to go to her." Mario sighed and looked up at the television on the wall. "It's like she wants me to be somebody else. Somebody I will never be."

"Like who?"

Mario looked at Devonte. "Like you."

Devonte nodded and his jaw twitched. "I don't know where you get that shit from but I would rather see her with you than somebody else."

"Even yourself?"

Devonte laughed. "Especially me," he replied. He raised his glass and Mario did the same. "To the family."

Mario slowly clinked his glass against his. "To the family." When they downed their drinks Mario asked, "So are you going to see your father or not? I overheard you talking to Lauren about the address Grams gave you."

Devonte shrugged. "First off he's not my father. He's some nigga who had something to do with my conception but that's about it." He sighed. "My grandmother keeps pressing me out but I'm playing it by ear."

A FEW WEEKS LATER

Devonte was lying on his living room floor with Tykisha riding his dick. Three other beauties were in attendance— Samantha, Eddie and Rebecca. He met Eddie and Rebecca the same night he reunited with Tykisha and they had been hanging around the Harrington family ever since.

As he fucked Tykisha's back out Eddie and Rebecca kissed one another in the corner of the room while Samantha lie on the floor playing with her pussy.

Just hearing Eddie and Rebecca fuck while Tykisha rode him caused his dick to harden even more. Tykisha's head dropped backwards as he pawned her breasts and a slight grin rested on his face. He was a long way from the kid nobody wanted and he wallowed in that thought every time he had more than one bitch at a time.

While Tykisha was getting her rocks off, Samantha hovered over Devonte's face and sat on it lightly. He loved nothing more than to eat pussy so she knew this would bring him closer to cumming. As his tongue flicked Samantha's clit four times, he could feel the nut pushing toward the tip of his dick. So he stiffened his tongue and rammed it inside her pussy hole as he pushed harder into Tykisha, exploding inside of her as if the levees on a dam broke.

When he was done Samantha eased off of him and Tykisha lowered her body and kissed his lips. She could taste the cream of another woman but it didn't matter. They had sex raw so many times if Samantha had a disease it meant they all did.

He smiled at Tykisha and smacked her right butt cheek. "Get up."

She rose and Tykisha grabbed his robe off of the sofa, handing it to him.

He put it on. "Make me something to eat, Samantha," he said.

Samantha hustled into the kitchen and Rebecca and Eddie followed.

Tykisha was about to help too but he stopped her. "I want you to look presentable tomorrow. Wear a nice dress or something."

She grinned and said, "Of course, God. What for?"

He wringed his hands. "I need you to take me somewhere."

She smiled feeling special. "Anything you want. All you have to do is ask."

CHAPTER NINE

God Of Gods

Devonte sat in the passenger seat of the car as Tykisha pulled up in front of the large church. When Devonte learned that his father was now a minister he couldn't believe it. But after a lot of research he found it was true. The man, who once didn't want anything to do with him, was now responsible for many.

Of course he would want to see his own son now.

Tykisha gazed out of the window at the beautiful church and said, "God, give me your piece," she paused pointing at the gun on his hip. "You don't want to take that up in there do you?"

He pulled out his .45, ejected the clip and handed it to her. She placed it under the front seat. "You know you don't have to do this right?" she continued. "We can pull off, maybe go to a restaurant and get something to eat."

He thought about his options and exhaled. "I didn't come here for nothing," he paused. "Let's go." He eased out of the truck and so did she. Taking his hand as if they were a happy couple they ascended up the steps.

She looked over at the designer black jeans, black shirt and gold chain and figured he was dressed appropriately enough.

As they walked, Devonte made several clicking noises before easing into the church. But instead of entering the nave, they stood in the vestibule entrance.

The moment he heard his father's voice, chills ran down his spine.

Tykisha on the other hand was in awe of his father. He and Devonte resembled so much they could be twins. Dipped in an all black suit, no preacher's robe, from the pulpit Eugene looked like a rock star.

A smile eased on Devonte's face as he realized how powerful his father had become. And within the vestibule, they listened to the rest of his fifteen-minute sermon, as Devonte remained anxious to meet him afterwards.

When service was over, Eugene Harrington, looked up and saw his only son watching with a beautiful woman standing next to his side. He stepped down shook a few hands and walked towards them.

After he finished with his congregation Eugene, with his son and Tykisha following, walked into his office. The moment the door slammed and they had privacy, the somber smile on Eugene's face diminished. "What the fuck are you doing here?"

Devonte stepped back, not believing he would react so coldly. "I...I was coming—"

"It doesn't matter." He examined Tykisha. "You and this little whore had better get out of my place of business."

"Hold up," she snapped.

"No, you hold up, young lady!" he roared. "This is my church and because of your creep show in the vestibule, I have to field questions from my members." He walked behind his desk and sat down. "The last

And They Call Me God

thing I need my congregation to think is that I had a kid by some dead junkie. And what's worse, that he brought his whore to church while wearing a fake diamond chain."

"Be glad we not strapped. I would've had your head blown off by now." He paused. "Fuck you, nigga."

Tykisha grabbed Devonte's hand and they stormed out of his office, pushing past the deacon who was on his way to greet Eugene.

When Devonte made it back outside he hopped into the truck, smacked Tykisha in the face and sat back in the seat. Instead of asking why she was struck she asked, "You need to do it again?"

He raised his hand and slapped her harder. Although she was in excruciating pain, she'd been with Devonte long enough to know how he reacted when his feelings were hurt. Her plan was to get into first place and she was willing to do whatever she had to.

"I'm sorry, God," she said pulling off.

Still enraged, Devonte removed his phone from his pocket. "Shaw, sell that property off Jefferson."

"You only got one property there. The one you gave to your grandmother."

His legs felt restless. "I know which one it is, nigga. Get it sold and let me know when it's done."

Devonte stood outside on his balcony overlooking Baltimore. His lips were wet from the vodka in the bottle that he was washing down his throat as humiliation on the earlier events replayed in his mind. Once again rejection made it clear that no matter how powerful he was, he was still a child wanting love and never having it returned.

"Can I get you anything?" Samantha asked walking outside. She felt a little dizzy as she approached, knowing how angry he was earlier. "Food? Sex? A dick suck?" she continued playfully.

Devonte focused on her and then turned his head toward the sparkling city. "No."

She moved closer, hands clutched in front of her. "I know you're use to being alone when you're angry. But when I got with the family, I made a decision that I would not leave your side, even during the tough times. I guess what I'm trying to say is that I'm here, God. Use me if you want to."

Devonte turned around and leaned against the guardrail. Adjusting his shades he raised the bottle and poured some more liquor down his throat. "You are under the impression that you anything other than a child to me. You're not my woman, Samantha, no matter how hard you try." He paused. "So I'm instructing you not to talk to me for the next 48 hours. You'd do wise to obey me."

As he was scolding her Lauren pushed the sliding door to the side, and passed Samantha to walk up to Devonte. She placed her cream Celine bag on the chair and stood in front of him. Her expensive perfume tickled his nostrils reminding him of yet another thing he couldn't have — her love.

Hugging Devonte with one arm she looked back at Samantha and asked, "Can you give us a little privacy?"

Samantha felt bitterness as she watched her standing next to him. Gazing at Devonte she waited for his word.

"Bounce," he told her.

And They Call Me God

Rolling her eyes, she stormed off of the balcony. In her absence Lauren focused on Devonte again who looked unraveled. "You don't look good, Devonte. You okay?"

Devonte turned toward the water, and raised his chin high as he washed more liquor down his throat. "Did you come here to lecture me or did you want something else?"

She crossed her arms over her body and tucked her hands under her armpits. "I wanted to tell you that me and Mario aren't going to make it." She looked out at Baltimore. "I don't love him...in that way at least. And I wanted to tell you because he has it in his mind that you and I are going behind his back."

Devonte sat the bottle down on the ground. His posture was stiff and his neck corded. Truthfully he didn't have time for the shit. "Come on, Lauren. Don't do this shit."

She dropped her hands down her sides, surprised that he was so concerned about her leaving Mario. "Don't do what? Not waste my time on someone I'm not interested in anymore?"

"Don't make a decision you might regret." He paused. "What other nigga in Baltimore gonna take care of you like you deserve? He's the one."

"Why are you so fucking sure?" she yelled.

"Because I made him in my image," he said in a hushed tone.

Her eyes widened in surprise. "Made him in your image?" she repeated. "Your arrogance never ceases to amaze me. What the fuck is that supposed to mean?"

Never being a man to return words he picked up the bottle again and said, "Just what I said." He took a swig. "Don't play dumb when you're a smart girl."

She nodded as if realizing something. "I don't know what games you're playing but you are really fucked up in the head. Sometimes I think you really believe your shit."

"Don't lose that nigga for some sucker who talking that soft shit in your ear."

"There's no other man! I'm in love with you, Devonte," she said heavily. "I don't know why because you act like you hate me. You use women's bodies as socks for your dick and you are hateful and scary. I'm telling you this not so you can leave to be with me. I would never want to hurt Mario in that way...but you...something about you..." she couldn't complete her sentence as the words exited her lips.

Devonte stepped up to her and said, "Lauren, I will never look at you like you want," he said softly. "Never," he continued. He felt himself getting emotional and pushed away from her. "Mario is for you...he'll treat you how you want and as long as I'm alive he will give you the world. If you leave him I will never talk to you again."

"So you're blackmailing me?"

Silence.

"If you feel so strongly about me why can't you treat me like I deserve?" she continued. She felt like a whore and a cheat the moment she allowed the words to flow from her lips. She was wearing Mario's ring and asking another man to express himself to her. But it was time to put everything on the line.

"Because I can't do anything but damage you even more." He felt the disappointment easing through his body. "And for the first time in my life I care too much about someone else to do that."

The sliding door flew open and Mario came rushing outside. "We been hit again," he said walking on the balcony. He was so scared about what happened that he didn't notice his woman and boss were too close.

Devonte and Lauren quickly separated.

"We gotta—" Finally realizing that Lauren was there he said, "I thought you were going over your friend's house."

She grabbed her purse. "I am over a friend's." She kissed Mario on the cheek, slid the door back and walked out, closing it behind her.

Confused, Mario watched her until she disappeared. "What was she doing here?" He asked.

"You know how Lauren is," Devonte took a swig of vodka and handed it to him, which he accepted. "But let's get back to business. What do you mean we been hit?"

"Some niggas walked into our stash again, the new one we just moved too." He paused. "It may be an inside job, God. I'm telling you, something feels off. The shit that's been happening lately has felt personal."

Devonte clicked his mouth a few times. "Who do you think it may be?"

"Varro," he said seriously.

Devonte laughed. "He's not crazy enough to make a move like that." He shook his head. "We just have to be smarter about where we keep our work until we get specific info."

Mario handed Devonte the bottle and stepped closer to the balcony, placing his hands on the rail. "How was the visit with your father?"

"Fuck that nigga." He paused as he waved at the air. "I feel like punching my grams in her face for convincing me to go see him." He took a large swig.

Mario shook his head. "You know Grams just want you to be happy, man. That's the only reason she gave you the address."

"Well I'm sick of that bitch being in my business." He took another gulp finishing the entire bottle before flinging it over the edge, not caring who he would hit below. "That's why I put that bitch out of the new house."

Mario threw his arms down the sides of his body and locked his hands into fists. "Threw her out? What the fuck you talking about?"

Devonte positioned himself so that they were face to face. "Just what I said."

Mario was too mad to know, but The Triad was watching his every move from the inside.

"What the fuck is wrong with you?" he asked. "One minute I think you're a good person and the next minute you do some shit like this! Don't you care about anybody but yourself?"

"You act like she's your grandmother."

Mario was done talking. He gritted on him and moved toward the door. "I don't know what your pops did to you. But this is the most heartless shit you ever did." He paused. "I'm done." He pushed the sliding door back and stormed away.

Devonte turned his body and inhaled the city. Although Mario chose to concern himself with his Grams, Devonte suddenly had a new idea to protect his stash that he couldn't wait to implement immediately.

CHAPTER TEN

The Manipulative One

Mario moved the final box into the bedroom in Aubrey's new apartment, which he set up and paid six months rent in advance. When he was done he walked into the kitchen where she prepared an Italian cold cut, fries and a cold glass of lemonade. Exhausted, he flopped onto the chair and wiped the sweat from his brow.

"I can't believe you had that much stuff in that house," Mario said. "Do you even use everything in this house?" he looked around.

She laughed and placed her hand on his shoulder before walking toward her teapot on the stove. "You collect a lot of stuff when you've lived as long as I have."

Mario grabbed the sandwich with soiled hands and stuffed his mouth. When he took a big bite, he placed the rest down. "I can't believe that nigga put you out of your other house," he said chewing with his mouth open. "It's been on my mind ever since I heard that shit."

She poured herself some coffee. "Don't be mad at Devonte," she sat next to Mario. "He's emotional right now over how my son treated him."

He muttered, "Fuck that nigga," under his breath but she heard him.

"Don't let him pull you into the darkness," she said softly. "Devonte has been through a lot and never learned the basics on how to treat other people."

Mario rolled his eyes. "Why does everyone take up for this dude? It's not emotional when you put your grandmother out on the street. It's cold blooded. Trust me, Grams. He's not the person you think he is."

She took a sip of coffee. "I might be old but I'm street wise. My grandson is exactly who I think he is." She paused. "And still there is a gentle side to him. Do you really believe he put me out and didn't feel turmoil?"

"All I know is when I drove by the block you were sitting on the chair with all of your things surrounding you. In the front yard of the house he just bought you." He paused. "He even had The Triad do it." Mario was so angry his face was reddening. "Them niggas went to the bar to get drunk because they felt so guilty afterwards."

"So then tell me this...how did you find out about me?"

He grabbed his sandwich and took another bite. "He told me."

"Exactly," she said tapping the top of his hand. "He told you because he knew you would come and help me. And you did. Devonte might be cold but beneath it all, he still knows love."

Mario was unrelenting. "I would've never done that to you."

"When a man is trapped in ego he may be liable to do things he normally wouldn't. Continue to be his friend because Devonte won't be here forever. And I rest easier at night knowing that he has you and Lauren around."

And They Call Me God

Eugene walked into his office after another Sunday service. When he opened the door he saw his mother sitting in his chair. With a stiff posture, she stood up and walked over to him. "When I found out about your church I praised God silently. Even told the ladies in my building that my son had turned his life over. I really thought you changed. Now I know that I was wrong."

He sighed, closed his door and walked toward her. "Get the fuck out of my office, mama." He flopped in his chair. "I have a business to run."

"You're the worse kind of man. The kind who dresses in the holy cloth while he still has disdain in his heart for people who come to him for relief."

"What are you talking about?"

"What man of God can actually hate his own son and still preach the word?"

He laughed at her. "You're playing right?" his tone was tart "You're the same person who did drugs before having me and while I was inside of you. And now that you're clean you expect me to listen to you? After you ruined my life and stole my childhood?" He moved a few papers around on his desk. "Get out of here, Aubrey, before I lay heavy hands on you."

She trembled. "You are right. I made mistakes. Lots of them. But what you have done by denying your only son last week has implications you cannot begin to fathom." She paused. "But as I look at you, I can tell that you don't even give a fuck."

Confused on what Devonte said was so important, Mario pulled up to an address Tykisha gave him earlier in the day. He rode past the location more than once because it led to a small church and he knew it had to be wrong. But on the third time he passed he leaned out the window and saw Devonte sitting on the steps of a closed church with The Triad standing behind him.

Mario parked his car and walked up the stairs leading to the tiny house of worship. He looked at the Triad and then down at Devonte. "What's going on, God?"

Devonte stood up, brushed off the back of his jeans and said, "Come inside. We have to show you something," he continued as he made clicking noises to the top.

Skeptical, Mario followed them. When he saw Devonte walking up the steps and onto the pulpit he thought it was a joke. "What do you think?" Devonte asked Mario with raised arms.

"Think about what?" Mario chuckled softly. "You joining a church now?"

"I'm running a church now," Devonte joked.

The Triad laughed too.

"Well, not in the conventional way," Devonte continued. "What we will be selling here will make people feel good instantly. And get this, they won't need their Bibles."

Mario felt the contents of his stomach flushing around. "I'm not understanding."

"From now on this is our new stash house. Within these walls we will maintain our dope and product. And they will never see us coming."

The Triad immediately grew excited. "Man, this move right here is the most genius shit you ever did,"

Greco responded rubbing his hands together. "Nobody will suspect us now."

"They'll never see us coming," Shaw responded as he flopped down in one of the pews.

"So it's ours?" Greco asked.

Devonte ran his hands over the paneling and imagined he was his father and had his own congregation. "The pastor who owned it can't afford the mortgage. Most of his members moved to other churches already. So for a few dollars a month he'll let us hold our community meetings here," he laughed. "At least that's what I told him."

Mario was so angry his hands clenched and unclenched in a pulsating manner. "Are you crazy?" Mario asked disgustedly. "Have you lost your mind?" he continued. "We can't sell dope in a place of worship."

"Yes we can," Devonte said loudly.

As Mario watched Devonte's ego transform he moved slowly toward the pulpit. "This is wrong, man. It's wrong. We better than this shit."

"You not even trying to give it a chance." Devonte stepped down and sat in one of the seats facing the pulpit and Mario sat next to him.

"We have to have limits, Devonte," he whispered. "Please, don't do this."

Devonte stood up. "I told you my name is God," he said firmly. "And I already made the deal. This is the best place to hide our work from unpaid cops and rivals. Either you in or I don't have any more use for you. It's your call."

Mario and Lauren were over Devonte's apartment helping him celebrate the new stash house. Although Mario was not with the concept, he used the opportunity to drink his guts out and clear his mind. Ever since he killed his cousin he couldn't hold his liquor, doing nothing but disgusting Lauren in the process.

Tykisha, on the other hand, sat on Devonte's lap and kissed him sloppily every time she saw Lauren looking their way. Tykisha was onto Lauren now and knew she wanted Devonte. The last thing she was going to do was allow that to happen.

Samantha, feeling out of place, pulled out the cocaine, which only made Lauren more uncomfortable. She grew even angrier when she looked around and saw everybody floating around as if everything was great in the world. Leaning closer to Mario she said, "Please don't do this tonight." She paused. "I was hoping we would go home early."

Frowning he said, "Fuck...for the first time in your life relax! I told you when we're married I'll stop. Until then I'm just a young nigga enjoying myself."

When Samantha separated the cocaine lines Mario grabbed a fifty-dollar bill and inhaled one. Since Lauren had known him he'd never tried hard drugs so she jumped up and moved toward the back of the loft.

"What's wrong with that bitch Lauren?" Tykisha whispered in Devonte's ear.

"Where she go?" he asked.

"The kitchen," she said covering her mouth with his.

Devonte squeezed the cheeks of her face together and said, "Never talk about her." He slapped her on the leg. "Now get up so I can see what's wrong."

He walked toward the kitchen and Lauren was pouring herself a glass of Sprite. When she saw Devonte she said, "I'm so sick of him." From where she stood behind the counter, she could see Mario getting higher than Rihanna's forehead. Her stomach twirled with disgust as she gazed at him. "This shit is all your fault."

"I don't do drugs," he responded.

"You just sit around while everybody else does them," she said shaking her head. Thinking about Mario she asked, "What have I gotten myself into?"

Devonte leaned up against the refrigerator. "He's just nervous about our new business venture that's all. Give him some time."

"What is it that has him so conflicted?" she asked.

"You know I will never tell you something that would put you in danger or trouble," he said.

She looked at Devonte. "It doesn't even matter. I'm done with him," she said under her breath.

Instead of dismissing her feelings he considered her energy. He clicked his tongue and pushed up on the back of her body. He had to see if she was as soft as he envisioned. Easing behind her he ran his hands down her shoulders, along her hips and down her thighs.

"What are you doing?" she whispered. "He may see you."

"That cocaine he's snorting is the best quality," he said. "The last thing he'll be thinking about is you right now."

In the past he wouldn't allow himself to consider her sexually but he had a lot on his mind and needed a release. With her back leaning against his chest, he lifted the black dress she was wearing that felt like a second skin under his fingertips.

By T. Styles 173

Removing his stiff penis, he pulled her panties to the side and eased into her pussy. She exhaled deeply as more and more of his long dick filled her up.

If Mario were to look their way, which he didn't, it would appear as if Devonte was standing behind her because the top counter concealed half of their head and the lower counter their lower body.

But Devonte wasn't just standing behind her. He was fucking her slowly, boldly and in the public while Mario snorted line after line of cocaine, never realizing he was losing the love of his life in the process.

As he melted into the flesh of her body he realized why Mario was tripping. Her pussy was tight, hot and pulsating.

Lauren was equally in awe at how they seemed to move so easily together. She envisioned having sex with Devonte many times but she never dreamed it would occur like this. Although they were not alone there was something alluring and bold in the way he chose to take her body. It was while Mario was in the house and not behind his back.

Devonte had three reasons for doing it this way.

First he wanted to know if she was really open for him the way she claimed. Second, he wanted to showcase his superiority over someone in light of how his father treated him.

Third, and the most important reason of all, he was falling in love.

"I'm going to call off the wedding," she said heavily as she watched Mario lean back in the sofa, head in the air. A line of blood eased from his nostril.

"Don't," he said as he felt himself about to cum. He gripped her hips and pounded harder.

She bit her bottom lip, filling herself about to cum also. "Then what do I do?"

And They Call Me God

"We'll figure out something," he said as he gripped her hips tighter and exploded inside of her.

When they were done she turned around, pulled her clothes down and gazed up at him. She could tell that he had no intentions of making her his own. "I don't want to be a part of the Harrington family, Devonte. I want you.," she said. "Either you want me or you don't. It ain't a lot to it."

"You're still engaged to Mario and in a crazy way he's family now."

"Is that why you just fucked me? Because he's your brother?" Her brows lowered. "I wish I'd never gave myself to you," she continued realizing the one thing you couldn't take back was pussy. "Stay out of my life and I'll stay out of yours." She stormed out of the kitchen, grabbed her purse, and left the apartment.

Mario was so high he didn't notice a thing.

CHAPTER ELEVEN

The Evil Has Arisen

2 MONTHS LATER

Five long metal tables filled with cocaine piles sat in the middle of the floor within the basement of the church, as twenty naked women packaged them in preparation for distribution.

Across the way, in a small courted off area, Devonte and The Triad were propped on leather sofas against the wall, with bottles of vodka on the table in front of them. It had been a long day. They just finished counting a half a million dollars in cash and was waiting on more profits to come in.

Preparing to discuss the business plan for the week, Greco ended the call he was on and placed his cell phone on the couch next to him. "Varro said he'll be here in fifteen minutes." He rubbed his hands through his smooth black hair. "Before I forget, God, do you know a boxer?" he paused. "The other night I saw some dude looking at us and talking to the bartender when we were at the strip club. When old boy left I asked the bartender what it was about and he said you."

Devonte leaned back. "I know a lot of people...not all of their professions though." He pushed his shades to his face. "Did the dude say what he wanted to the bartender?"

"I was there that night too," Shaw added. "He didn't say what he wanted but I got the impression that he was definitely interested in doing you harm." He paused. "We chased the nigga outside but he got away."

Since a stranger asking questions about a drug boss always brought about anxiety, Devonte grew uncomfortable. "Just keep eyes out for him. We can't give all of our attention to a ghost we know nothing of."

Shaw fired up a joint and passed it around.

"So what's up with the new boy?" Greco questioned.

"What you talking about?" Devonte asked grabbing the weed when it was handed to him. He pulled and passed it around again.

"He always here for payday but never deals with the risk," he responded. The liquor had him feeling too comfortable around God, which was a big mistake. "If you ask me it ain't fair."

Devonte shot him a glare that he wouldn't soon forget. "Who's asking?"

Silence.

"Don't ever come at me about my associates," Devonte continued. "What happens between me and a anybody I break bread with is my business."

Everybody present thought Devonte's dog was off leash but what else could they say?

"What's going on?" Mario asked stepping up to them. He was holding a brown paper bag filled with whiskey. Lately he didn't do too many things without a bottle in hand, and that included handling business for the family. "Why everybody so uptight?"

"Why you covered in blood?" Greco snapped.

Mario glanced down at his clothes and said, "My bitch got her period and it splashed on me when I fucked her from the back," he joked.

Devonte got up and touched Mario on his shoulder. "Come with me."

Mario took a look back at The Triad again and followed Devonte. They walked into a small office no bigger than a closet but large enough for a private meeting. The moment the door closed Devonte got straight to the point. "You washed up, man. You haven't been yourself and people who've known me longer are starting to question my authority."

Mario's neck wobbled backwards. "I still do my job, God. What difference do it make if I drink a little?"

"I think you got shit fucked up, slim." Devonte said as he breathed heavily through his nose. "This is a business. And so you could keep your bitch I allowed you along for the ride. Don't fuck up."

"Ohhhhhh….she's a bitch now?" he asked taking another swig. "Because I thought she was the girl you wanted to fuck."

Devonte started to tell him he already had her. But even though he hadn't spoken to Lauren he cared about her too much to disrespect. "I'm sick of you coming at me about that bitch. Either you get with what we have going on here or you're cut. We need your head in the game. Niggas are circling me and shit is getting tight."

"What happened between you two?" Mario asked getting back on Lauren.

"This is about business," Devonte reminded him.

"So you not gonna answer my question?" he paused. "How come she hasn't been talking to you? Why every time I bring up your name she gets upset? What the fuck happened that you not telling me?"

Devonte stepped so close to Mario that he was backed into the wall and unable to move. "From here on out, when it comes to that bitch, don't ask me shit." He paused. "If I wanted her I could've had her and you would be an afterthought. You're weak and scared and I'm tired of babysitting."

Mario tried to wiggle from around him but Devonte wouldn't budge. "Whatever," Mario said under his breath.

Devonte was about to crash the back of his skull but he had grown to care about him and it complicated their relationship even more.

When there was a knock at the door Devonte said, "Come in."

It was Greco. "Just got word that somebody murdered Varro in his car while sitting in front of his mother's house," he said. "I got a few men checking on him now."

Mario took a swig of his liquor, smiled and walked out.

Devonte sat in the backseat of a black Ford Crown Victoria. Tykisha sat next to him while Greco drove. The only thing on Devonte's mind was whether or not Mario was capable of murder— a second time. If it were true Mario was not the punk he thought and he would have to watch him closely or be caught.

When Greco and Devonte questioned him about Varro's murder he swore he wasn't responsible.

No one believed him.

He was wearing the evidence on his clothes.

When Greco pulled up on the left side of a grey ford truck, a black Caprice with tinted windows pulled up on the right. In sync, both vehicles rolled their windows down and fired into the car.

"What the fuck!" Greco said as he ducked down and pressed the gas pedal so hard his toe broke. He raised his shirt, removed the .9 mm from his waist and fired out of the shattered window. "Get down, God!"

Devonte and Tykisha had already crouched down while the shooters in separate vehicles unloaded into the Crown Vic, shattering the windows.

Tykisha managed to reach her purse and grab her .45. When she was loaded she rose and fired on the right while Greco unleashed on the left.

To Devonte things appeared to move in slow motion. Who was trying to kill him? Was it his good friend, Mario?

Although frightened, Tykisha stuck her head out of the broken window and fired at the gunmen behind the Crown Vic. Her aim was so accurate, that she managed to shoot one of the drivers in his shoulder, causing the car to spiral into another car behind it.

Now they only had the truck to worry about.

Greco, while maintaining control of the steering wheel, was shooting out of the window on the left. He looked back frequently to be sure Devonte was okay and he was.

Shards of glass covered everything inside and suddenly another gunshot flew into the right side of the Crown Vic ripping into Greco's arm.

"I'm hit!" he screamed out.

The car swerved wildly before he regained control with his good hand. But he could no longer keep the car off of their trail. It was Tykisha who was going to need to handle business.

And They Call Me God

"Fuck this shit," she yelled reloading. "Stop the car, Greco. Let me light into these niggas!"

"Are you crazy?" he screamed looking at her from the rearview mirror. "We can't be slowing down."

"I didn't say slow down, I said stop!"

Greco looked back at her and said, "Fuck it. Let's handle our business."

Pulling over to the side of the road Tykisha jumped out. The gunmen were surprised the car stopped and even more surprised that a female was aiming at them with a gun.

With precision she got into the middle of the street and fired, hitting the driver in the throat. The truck swerved and slammed into an electrical pole.

When her work was done Tykisha jumped back in the car and said, "I got 'em!" she looked out of the back window. "Let's get out of here!"

Devonte sat on the seat, glass stabbing into his buttocks. Now he wanted blood.

But whose?

Devonte stood on his balcony, still covered in Greco's blood. Breathing in and out he was trying his best to calm himself down but nothing worked. If it were true that Mario tried to kill him, he would not give him another chance to be successful.

The first thing Devonte did was get Greco to the hospital so the bullet could be removed from his arm and a splinter placed on his toe. Afterwards he beefed up security at the house, allowing only The Triad, Samantha and Tykisha to be around.

After hearing what happened to the family, the new girls Eddie and Rebecca attempted to visit but The Triad vetoed their request. They could trust no one so they were not allowed in.

Devonte picked up his bottle of vodka on the table and swallowed it halfway down. Darby, one of his new soldiers, slid the door to the side and entered. "God, Lauren is here. You want me to send her back?"

"Move," Lauren said shoving past Darby and making her way onto the balcony. She rushed up to Devonte and when she saw Greco's blood over his body her stomached bubbled. "Oh my, you could've been...you could've been..."

"I could've been nothing," he said calmly. "Not even bullets whirling past my head could penetrate the God." He beat his chest. "Now what the fuck do you want?"

With confused eyes she tried to determine if he was serious or not. Could he really be that delusional? When she first heard that Greco was hit and that Devonte was in the car with him, she realized not talking to him was dumb. But now, as she stood in front of him, bearing witness to his arrogance, she was disgusted.

"What are you talking about? Do you actually think that just because you call yourself God that you are one?" she paused. "And that you can't be killed? You're not immortal, Devonte. God doesn't shit, eat or breathe!"

"You got five minutes to tell me what the fuck you want."

She wiped the tears streaming down her face. "I was worried. The moment I thought something happened to you I couldn't even hold down air. And now you're acting like...you're acting like ...you don't care."

"Why can't you see that I'm not one of them little niggas chasing behind you? I came in this world alone and I'm gonna leave that way." He paused. "Go home." he waved her off and swallowed some more vodka. "What you need to be doing is checking for that nigga of yours, instead of worrying about me. My point four five has a bullet with his name on it and his time is numbered."

Sensing that he believed Mario was responsible for the shoot out, caused her stomach to be more upset. With wide eyes she asked, "You can't possibly think Mario was involved with this—"

"Get the fuck out of my house!"

"Devonte—"

"God!" he said correcting her. "You've taken too many
liberties with my name. You won't take another. Now bounce!"

His booming voice caused her to shiver and for a moment she remained still. Not recognizing him anymore, slowly she backed out of the balcony before leaving the apartment.

"Darby," Devonte yelled placing his hands on the banister.

Darby hustled to greet him. "Yes, sir."

"Bring me a beer, and tell the girls to leave me alone."

"Right away, sir," he said.

When the beer was brought back Devonte put down the vodka and cracked it open. "Come closer," he said. Devonte could feel his shaky breaths on his neck. "You had one job." He took a large sip. "Not to let anybody in my house except who was on the list. And you failed."

Before Darby could respond Devonte picked him up and shoved him over the edge so quickly he didn't see it coming. As he screamed on the way to the ground, Tykisha, Samantha and The Triad rushed outside, thinking God was in trouble.

"Call the ambulance," he said calmly. "The nigga Darby just took a dive."

CHAPTER TWELVE

Married To The Dream

L auren stood in front of a mirror with Rebecca and Eddie standing behind her as she wore a beautiful wedding gown in a boutique. It was pearl colored, with shimmering beads along the side and it looked like it was made for a star. The back of the gown was split all the way to the cup of her lower back, revealing her sleek curves. She looked stunning and yet she was far from a happy bride.

After Greco was shot Devonte limited the amount of people that hung around him which meant Rebecca and Eddie, who forged a small bond with Lauren, for the moment were out of the mix.

"You look beautiful and sad," Rebecca said softly as she gazed at Lauren's reflection in the mirror. "You're about to be a bride, why aren't you smiling?"

Lauren took a deep breath, turned around and gazed at them. "Can you promise me you'll watch after him?" she paused. "Devonte?"

Rebecca lightly stroked Lauren's arm. "You act like you're going to be out of his life."

"I am," she picked up the edge of her dress and stepped off the wooden block. "He wanted it that way and I'm not fighting with him anymore." She removed the dress and an assistant took it to the back. Standing in her pink bra and panties set she realized she dropped more weight than she wanted.

"You love him don't you?" Eddie asked.

"I care about him."

"Why don't you tell him how much?" Rebecca asked. "Don't marry a man you don't care about in that way. Call the wedding off with Mario."

"There's a lot about Devonte that you don't know," Lauren said sliding into her t-shirt. "Loving him is not that easy."

"Do you know anything about Darby falling off of the balcony last night?" Eddie asked.

"No," she sighed. "He was there when I left and then I found out through the streets that he fell."

"Do you believe it?" Rebecca asked as if taking mental notes.

Something about the third degree she was giving made her uncomfortable. "I believe him," she responded. "Devonte may be mean but he's not a murderer," she lied, knowing he was capable.

"Well, you would know," Eddie said sitting down. "How long have you two been friends?"

Lauren eyed Rebecca and Eddie closely. Now that she looked at them they seemed different and she didn't want to be around them anymore. "Look, I have to go," Lauren said. "I didn't realize how late it was. I'll get up with you two later." She grabbed her purse and walked out the door.

Mario sat at the table with Lauren eating spaghetti for dinner. He made several attempts to hold basic conversation with her that evening but she was cold and aloof. Irritated he asked, "How did your wedding gown fit?" he grabbed a piece of garlic bread and chewed it mouth open like a cow. "I bet that ass looks good in it."

"It fit nicely, Mario", she said with a slight attitude. She forked her food.

"Do you need alterations?" he paused. Wanting to say something to get an emotional rise he said, "I see you put on a little weight."

"You see I put on a little weight?" she laughed. "I lost over fifteen pounds since I've been with you. But what about you? Posted up like an old drunk with ruffle britches."

He leaned back into his seat, grabbed the whiskey bottle on the table and looked over at her. "You've changed."

"Why?" she said sarcastically. "Because I'm not playing sleep while you jack off on my ass anymore?" she laughed. When she saw the surprised look on his face she said, "Yes, nigga...I was awake that night. You were a pervert then and you a hotter mess now."

Embarrassed, he walked to the bar, made himself a drink and looked over at her.

"Did you have anything to do with Devonte almost being shot?" she asked squinting.

His eyes widened and he placed the glass of vodka down. "You would really ask me some shit like that?"

Silence.

"You didn't come up with the idea on your own though did you? You can't do anything on your own." he paused. "He put that shit in your head and you believed him." he waved dismissively. "I'm sure you probably already sucked the nigga's dick by now."

"I hate you!" She yelled. "I wish I never said yes!"

"I'm sure you do...but you love Devonte don't you?" He chuckled although he'd rather cry. "Always have and always will."

Mario looked down at her. "If you ever ask me something like that again it won't be healthy." He grabbed the bottle of vodka off the bar and stormed out of the apartment.

Mario hugged Aubrey as he entered her apartment. She pulled her robe closed and said, "I'm happy to see you, son," she paused but observed his shaky physique. "After you left the last time I saw you I was concerned. Where have you been?"

Mario, drunk out of his mind, stared at her for a second as if he was contemplating doing her bodily harm. After all, she was Devonte's grandmother.

If he hurt her hard enough would he care?

His lips were wet with liquor and his energy made her uncomfortable. She tapped at her housecoat to make sure her nine milli was at her side...and it was.

"I've been around," he said burping. "Out of respect I didn't come earlier like I wanted."

"Out of respect?" she paused. "You talk as if we aren't family."

He leaned against the wall by the door. "We aren't, Aubrey", he said walking to the sofa and flopping down. "Family doesn't try to kill each other. Family doesn't blame each other for things they didn't do. And family doesn't destroy relationships."

Aubrey walked up to him and sat down. Placing a soft hand on his thigh she noticed he was trembling. "I don't know what's going on with you and Devonte but I know he cares about you. The rest of them latched on to hide under the power they thought he possessed.

You two came afterwards and I sensed he was better with you in the picture."

"You mean he took us on as pet projects."

"That's not what I meant."

Mario looked down at his hands and then at her. "I won't be coming back to see you. And I wanted to say goodbye personally."

Her eyes widened. "Honey, don't say that."

"I'm telling you the truth. This will be my last time. And I'm here now so that you can know how much I appreciate everything you've done for Lauren and me. I don't know my family well and you always made me feel at home."

She stroked his curly sweaty hair backwards. "It doesn't have to change."

"It's not changing because it was never real. You are his grandmother not mine. I think I allowed myself to get too comfortable because I didn't want to see the truth about me and Devonte's relationship. It's built on the illusion called Lauren. But I'm not blind anymore." He stood up and she did too.

"Son —"

"There's nothing to be said," he fumbled toward the door. "Me and Devonte have turned enemy and that makes you enemy blood." He walked out leaving Aubrey stunned.

Devonte sat in his church with Detective Rothersburg and Detective Kona. A bottle of vodka sat on the floor and each had a plastic cup filled with liquor in their hands. Although they were different —

Devonte a criminal and them officers, they were enjoying themselves as if they were good friends.

"I got to admit," Rothersburg said as he looked at the pulpit. "This is your best idea yet, Devonte." He took a huge sip from his cup.

Devonte's chest poked out proudly. "Yeah...now that I have this place, and it's off the radar, I get to move my work in secret." He paused. "I can even make enough to pay you greedy mothafuckas," he laughed.

"You are virtually off the radar with this spot," Kona added. "How did you come across it?"

"It dropped in my lap," he said. "The old preacher running it couldn't afford the mortgage so I took it off his hands." he dug into his pocket and handed Kona a stack of one hundred dollar bills. "Thanks for staying off my back."

"You pay to play," Rothersburg said. "This is no favor. It's business."

Kona handed the money to Rothersburg and the mood grew dark. "I'm going to tell you something because I think it's serious," Rothersburg said. "You are being hunted."

"Hunted?" he replied. "By who?"

Kona dug into his pocket and removed a paper before reading the name. "Do you know a Stanford Collins?" he paused. "A professional MMA boxer out of Baltimore."

Immediately what Devonte did to him in the shower when he was a kid came to mind. It was a moment he regretted and one he hoped wouldn't come back to haunt him.

It did.

"What he want with me?" he asked as if he didn't know.

"Not sure...just letting you know," Kona said. "You're not worried are you?"

Devonte tried to play big but there was nothing like an enemy with a serious vendetta to get the heart going. "All I have to do is throw some money on the matter and it will disappear. I'm not worried."

The situation was turning ugly. "Money can't buy everything," Rothersburg said.

"You sure about that?" Devonte responded sarcastically.

"Don't get arrogant, nigger," Kona responded thinking he was referring to them. "We take your money because we can, not because you own us."

Devonte laughed. "Say whatever you need to get you to sleep at night. Just know that because of me, you both have shiny new Benzes sitting on the curb." He paused. "You can kiss the ring later."

"I'm gonna pretend you didn't say that shit," Rothersburg said.

Kona laughed. "We like you, Devonte," he said. "Always have. But your arrogance will be the fall of your empire." He looked up at the stain glass windows. "If that's what you want to call this abomination."

"When you've come as far as I have you can't fall. And you find that you can get anything you want with a fan of a few hundred dollar bills."

Kona and Rothersburg stood up and looked down at Devonte, reminding him for a moment that they were the law. "The girl you love but could never have is at the X Club," Kona said. "She looked pretty lonely and whorish. It would be a shame for me to slide up on her and give her some of this good white cock. The sisters do have a thing for white masters you know?"

They both walked toward the exit. "Ten to one that you won't last in this place," Rothersburg said as they continued to walk out.

"I'll take those odds," Devonte said quietly as he turned around and listened to them leave.

Lauren's hips swerved slowly in a wave like motion, as her arms were raised in the air sensuously. Sweat poured down her shoulders as she made a decision to dance her problems away.

The pink top she wore exposed just enough cleavage and the black pants squeezed her curves. Lauren had the attention of every man in the club and none of them were right. Finally after watching her seduce every man present, Greco, with his arm in a sling, pulled himself from the darkness and approached her. "You finished?" he asked softly.

She turned around and looked up at him, knowing he was there for Devonte. "Tell him to leave me alone," she said facing the opposite direction. "He's done with me and I'm done with him."

"He's not going to do that, Lauren." His voice was heavy with bass because his lips were inches away from her ear. "So stop playing games before I snatch you." His arm was in a sling and his toe in a splint but he would've yanked her with the quickness.

Not wanting to be humiliated, Greco led her off the floor and into the VIP section of the club where Devonte sat tucked in the corner. "You enjoying yourself?" he asked the moment he smelled her perfume.

"What do you want?" She responded.

"To buy you one more drink," he said. "Can you have one more drink with a good friend?"

"I think we should keep shit professional," she said harshly.

"You don't sound right," he said. "A girl who's getting married should feel more excited than you."

"I'm so tired of people saying that shit," she yelled.

"I care, Lauren."

"Like you really give a fuck."

"I always give a fuck about you. Just because it doesn't look like love doesn't mean its not."

She sat next to him mainly because her feet hurt. "Devonte, please leave me alone. I'm tired of the mental seesaw. I just can't take it anymore."

He touched her shoulder. "I was just coming by to say I'm sorry, Lauren. For how I treated you and Mario." He paused. "I'm done with the beefing shit. I had a wakeup call tonight and my plan is to settle down and maybe even have a few kids."

She laughed. "And when is this supposed to go down?"

"After I tuck a little money away and put the dope game behind me."

"Why are you telling me this?"

"Because you were right about me," he said seriously. "You were always right. I've been selfish lately and maybe I didn't want to hear it at first."

She finally turned to look at him and her heart skipped when she saw how handsome he was. Even with his shades on she felt his eyes were penetrating her soul. The seat of her panties moistened from thoughts of their sexual encounter together although brief. "So how are you going to settle down? With two or four of your bitches?"

"I'm going to ask Tykisha to marry me." He paused. "I know I don't love her in that way. But she put it all on the line the other day when Greco was shot. She risked her life for me and maybe it's time to start taking her seriously."

Lauren felt as if she'd been gut punched. She didn't know what she expected him to say but it certainly wasn't that "You don't know what you want?"

Lauren felt herself about to cry and it was difficult to look at him anymore. "I'm not going to lie, Devonte. Hearing that you've chosen her hurts my feelings but I want you to be happy. More than anything I want you to have peace. "

Devonte moved closer. "I'm sorry about what I did to you in the kitchen. You deserve better than me treating you like some whore. I hope that someday you'll forgive me." He kissed her on the head, stood up and walked out.

Right before The Triad took him to his car, Lauren rushed out of the club and up to him. She grabbed his hand and The Triad touched the handle of their weapons as if unsure of her motives.

Breathing heavily she said, "Watch Rebecca and Eddie. I don't trust them."

He smiled, pulled her close and kissed her on the lips. Afterwards he released her hand and eased into the Escalade.

It was as if he already knew.

CHAPTER THIRTEEN

Nudge The Beehive

Stanford stood in the middle of the park waiting for his cousin Harper who was supposed to be helping him fuck up Devonte's life. After Harper conducted the missed hit on Devonte, when Tykisha and Greco got into a successful shoot out with them, Stanford realized things were more serious than he thought.

Ninny rushed up to him. "I looked everywhere," she said breathing heavily. Her complexion reddening. "I don't see Harper's car."

Although Stanford didn't have a relationship with Harper and his other family after Devonte raped him, he guilted Harper into helping. In his mind, the one action of denying Devonte the invite to the party at Dove's Home For Boys was the cause of Stanford's world crumbling down. Although petty, at the center of Stanford's belief system, he also couldn't shake that his life changed that day. At the end of the day Harper's jealousy catapulted a series of events that crushed Stanford's childhood.

After hearing that Harper was nowhere to be found Stanford paced in place. His eyes wide and bulging. When he stopped he looked directly into Ninny's eyes. "Something is wrong."

Ninny walked closer. "What do you mean?"

Stanford breathed heavily and then stopped suddenly as if he passed out while standing up. "He knows," he sighed. "Devonte knows we're after him."

Devonte sat in the backseat of a slow moving Extended Escalade with Harper, the man who killed Heather and attempted to take his life. They dressed him in a yellow raincoat, with his hands tied behind his back, and he didn't know what was about to happen.

"I'm ready, Greco," Devonte said calmly. He was sitting in the passenger seat while Chicago was perched in the driver's seat. A few seconds later he brought the car to a slow crawl in a residential area of Baltimore.

This meeting was a long time coming. After scouring the town for the shooter, dropping a few thousand to snitches in the process, he finally learned who was responsible for Heather's death and the recent shoot-out. In the scheme of Devonte's life he had forgotten all about Stanford and Dove's Home For Boys. But they never forgot about him.

Chicago pulled in front of a row house in Baltimore and Harper trembled, recognizing the place. He looked over at Devonte. "Please don't do this, man. I didn't even want to get involved in this shit. Stanford pulled me in."

Devonte laughed. "Why should I grant you mercy? What have you given me? You killed someone in my family and you had something to do with the night my life changed. At the school."

Harper's life was on speed, and he'd done so much grime, that he had no idea what he was talking about.

"I promise you I don't know what you're talking about."

"The last night I saw you, at Dove's School. You didn't like me. Why?"

Greco and Chicago looked at one another, having no idea that this hate reached deeper than the roots of a fifty-year-old oak tree.

Harper slowed his breaths and tried his hardest to consider what he was talking about. He felt his life depended on saying the right thing. After pulling a small memory of the time in Dove's from his database he said, "I guess I didn't like you because you were harder than me at that time."

"I'm harder than you now, nigga," God said. "Now explain yourself."

"I was afraid to do some of the things you did. And I resented you for being able to do them."

"So you rejected me because you were weak?"

Silence.

Devonte leaned his head back in his seat. "In later years, a lot of people got hurt by me because of that one night," Devonte said in a whisper. "I guess you never know what will set a nigga off do you?" He paused. "Unfortunately I can't grant you mercy."

"Listen, I...I didn't want to kill the white girl but-"

"You did it anyway," Devonte said.

Harper's eyes darted around the truck. "I will do anything you want." He paused. "Even suck your dick."

Upon hearing the comment, Chicago released himself out of the driver's side, walked around to where Harper sat, grabbed the front of the raincoat, stole him in the nose twice and closed the door.

When Chicago eased back into his seat, Harper realized their stance on his oral sex suggestion. In Harper's defense he knew his cousin was raped by

Devonte and didn't understand that Devonte's process was for humiliation purposes, not sexual satisfaction or attraction. Although most men would be just as confused.

"Where is Stanford?" Devonte asked pressing the shades back to his face.

Harper wiped the blood away from his upper lip, that streamed from his throbbing nose and said, "I told you everything I know, man. He meets us at a park before he pays us. He's my cousin but I don't know if he lives in Baltimore or out of state."

Devonte turned his head toward Greco who removed a cell phone from his pocket, whispered inside of it and ended the call.

"Look out the window," Devonte said to Harper, although he himself kept his head toward the front of the truck.

Harper looked over Devonte and at the house. The curtain of the window was pushed back and Harper saw his ten-year-old son being pressed against the glass and his face splattered. Upon seeing the horrible sight, Harper immediately went faint, unable to take in what he just witnessed.

"I wanted that to be the last thing you saw. I figured the window would be a good point, seeing as how you looked snidely at me before crawling out of one the last time I saw you." Devonte removed a .45, clicked his tongue a few times and shot Harper in the face. The raincoat he wore caught most of the blood matter, preventing the seats from being totally drenched in blood.

Greco got out, opened Harper's door and dragged the body to the ground. Easing back into the truck, Greco looked back at Devonte. "Where next, God?"

And They Call Me God

"I know exactly where Stanford is," Devonte said confidently. "I should've gone there a long time ago."

Dove's Home For Boys had been abandoned for three years after a group of children kept twenty employees hostage due to unfair conditions. Instead of letting them go, the boys killed them one by one, before turning the weapons on themselves.

When the investigation got underway, the government learned there was more going on in the home then they were aware of. From extortion to child abuse, Dove's was a haven for the most deprived and the children leaving the property were always changed for the worst. A decision to shut it down immediately was reached.

After hearing what happened to Harper, Stanford decided to finish Devonte after he developed another plan. For the time being all he wanted to do was leave Baltimore and recoup.

Trying to get away, Stanford rushed into the same room he and Devonte lived in when they were kids. Ninny was busy getting a rental car so that they could leave town immediately.

When he turned the light on, which was nothing more than a candle he lit, the room illuminated with Devonte standing in the corner— Greco and Chicago were behind him.

"Going somewhere?" Devonte asked calmly.

Stanford paced jerkily, before stopping and placing his hands on his hips. "You had this coming," Stanford finally said leaning against the wall. "You don't...I did this because you don't take a man's pride and then..."

"The product of one evil is not to blame for the product of another. In a world of monsters only the strongest survive. That night in the shower it was me. If you were smarter, this night could've been yours."

Stanford's heart beat rapidly although he acted as if he were in control. "Let me go, man," he said calmly. "I'm leaving Baltimore. I'm done with this shit and you'll never hear from me again."

Devonte laughed. "I can't do that," he paused. "I need my enemies to rest in peace before I do."

"So you don't have no shame about what you did to me in this place?"

"I'm incapable of shame. These days I'm incapable of compassion too."

Realizing there was nothing he could say, Stanford pulled himself off the wall and started shadow boxing. Chicago and Greco stepped in front Devonte, although allowing Stanford the honor of going out swinging.

After a few more seconds, Devonte clicked his tongue several times and Greco and Chicago lit Stanford's body up like the Las Vegas strip.

✝

Devonte seemed to sink deeper into the cushions of his grandmother's sofa. He was aware that the new place Mario moved her to was smaller, but something about the energy of it made him feel at home.

Aubrey sat next to him and touched his leg. Looking upon him lovingly she said, "You look bad, Devonte. Worse than I've ever seen you."

"Such is life," he smiled pressing the shades back toward his face. He sat up straight and clasped his hands together on his knees. "So how are you?"

"I'm good," she said softly. He seemed off and she didn't know if she should be afraid of him or concerned. "I'm more worried about you. If I knew you were safe I would be able to get more sleep."

He nodded and leaned back again. It was as if he were exhausted.

"Son, what is wrong?" she persisted. "Talk to me."

Devonte turned his head in her direction. "I'm sorry...for what I did to you. You didn't deserve being put out on the streets."

"It's okay I know you—"

He raised his hand, silencing her before dropping it on his lap. "I don't understand why you sent me to him when you knew what kind of person he was."

"Do you really think if I knew he would hurt your feelings that I would've told you to go see him?"

"Nobody hurt my feelings!" he yelled.

"I'm sorry," she paused. "I didn't mean it that way." She swallowed. "I wanted you to find what you are searching for. I wanted you to find closure."

Devonte's mind was suddenly filled with incoherent whispers. He stood, clicked his tongue and paced. "I don't know what that means...I don't know how to be okay with niggas who were supposed to care about me leaving me out in the cold! I don't know how to accept my mother and father not wanting me! Or my aunt abandoning me when I needed her most." He paused, breathing heavily. "And every time I try to let go, a new piece of concrete covers my heart making it even harder to give a fuck!" he panted heavily. "I'm just a used up nigga who can't even—"

"Can't even what, son?"

Silence.

"Son…what can't you do?" she asked again.

When he didn't respond she rose, walked toward him and slowly she reached out and touched his hand. He allowed her but was as stiff as an animal backed up in a corner. One wrong move and she was sure he would attack.

Boldly placing her hand over his heart she said, "let go of it, Devonte." She paused. "Let go of it. The pain is sitting on the surface, ready to free itself from your life. Give it the honor and let it go. You'll be free…I swear it!"

Breathing heavily he said, "Do you believe, do you really believe that you can be forgiven for the things you've done, when you would do them all over again if given a chance?"

She released his hand, and slowly raised her hands to remove his shades. When she looked into his eyes it was as if she was gut punched. Sensing she was on to him, he snatched his glasses, clicked his tongue a few times and ran out of her apartment where The Triad was waiting outside of the door.

Nothing more than an emotional mess, Lauren drove down the block, with her heart in her pockets. She was supposed to be getting married the next day and finally came to terms with it being off.

She got out of her car and walked to her front door but when she did, she could feel somebody standing behind her. Her body trembled before she even turned around. "Don't look back here, bitch," a man said. "Just open the door and—"

And They Call Me God

His sentence was cut off when a bullet penetrated his head and he was killed. Lauren turned around, the back of her body drenched with his blood. She looked for the shooter. Where had the shot come from? When she glanced down and saw a man she didn't know spread out on the ground in front of her house, she snatched the keys out opened the door and ran inside.

Slamming the door behind herself, she dropped her purse on the floor and backed inside, staring at the door the entire time. "Mario somebody just tried to kill me!" she yelled, hoping he would come out and help her. When he didn't she ran through the house. When she realized he wasn't home, she sat on the sofa, pulled her knees to her chest and called Devonte. The phone rang once before he finally answered. Frantically she said, "Devonte, somebody, somebody just tried to..."

"Lauren, slow down," he said calmly.

"I can't! Somebody just tried to kill me! But...but...before he did..."

Her gaze darted from the door and various areas in the house. It was as if she was afraid the objects around her would transform into masked gunmen. She was going crazy. "I know, Lauren."

Her eyes widened and she tightened her grip on the phone. Trembling she asked, "What do you mean you know?"

"I know somebody tried to kill you." He paused. "And don't worry about the body. It's being taken care of right now. Just keep the windows closed and stay in the house. You are being looked after even now."

"I don't understand."

"After what happened to me in the car, and with Heather being murdered, I have someone following you." He paused. "At all times."

"What the fuck you mean you have someone following me? What is wrong with you, Devonte? How could you involve me in this shit?"

"Lauren, the moment you accepted the dough you became involved in this lifestyle," he paused. "The only thing I'm doing is protecting you and making sure you're safe." Upon hearing that she was not appreciative, his ego rose to his defense. "Instead of coming at me hard you should be on your knees sucking my dick! I saved your life! Again!"

She shook her head. "I should've known that all the shit you pulled at the club was an act." She paused. "You don't love people. You own possessions with souls and I'm not one of them."

"If that's how you feel I'll leave you to it, Lauren. But I did a lot of clean up work over the past few days. Anybody who wanted to come at me was taken care of tonight. I only have one enemy alive and you're fucking him."

"You mean yourself?" she said sarcastically knowing she threw him a shot of pussy one night.

"Nah, shawty, I'm talking about the nigga you're fucking on the regular."

"So you're trying to say Mario would try to…would try too…"

"You were with me at the bar, Lauren. And you know how he feels about our friendship. Plus I didn't want to tell you but Varro's murder was no accident. Open your eyes and look at your man. You'll see I'm not the only monster in your circle."

"Bye, Devonte!" she hung up and leaned back into the sofa. Her anxiety was so high that she almost couldn't breathe. When the call was ended Mario walked inside and she looked at him as if she didn't know him. After all…did she?

"Baby, what you spill that was red outside of the house?"

"Spill?" she asked. "You didn't see...anything else?"

"Anything like what?" he asked confused.

A body. She thought.

Lauren considered what Devonte said about Varro. "Let me ask you something...do you know what happened to Varro?"

He laughed. "Yes."

Her eyes widened and her breaths quickened. "So you did kill him?"

"I said I know what happened to him," he responded coyly. "But we all do. It's been on the news." He smiled wider. "Why? They found the nigga who shot him yet?" he paused. "Because I doubt they will. He's probably long gone by now. Too smart to be apprehended by average cops."

She didn't recognize the man standing before her. He was becoming more unraveled and she was certain that he killed him. "Mario, would you ever try to hurt me?"

He laughed and walked closer. "Hurt you? Why would you even ask me that?"

"Answer the question."

"Lauren, I have loved you from the first time I saw your face. I would never try to hurt you purposely."

She sighed, and looked into his eyes. "I can't marry you, Mario."

"What do you mean you can't marry me?"

"I can't do this with us anymore. I don't...I don't love you in that way. If we try hard enough, maybe we can go back to our friendship."

He had an emotionally choked face. "I don't know what's going on but now is not the time to be pulling this shit. I just put everything I had on this wedding

By T. Styles   205

because you said you wanted it. And now you want to just walk away?" He approached her preparing to lay hands on her. He resembled a rabid animal that was looking for a reason to chew her apart.

Right before he laid his hands on her she remembered something Devonte said. "Look out of the window, Mario," she said quietly.

"For what?" he asked, teeth bearing, preparing to rip into her.

"Just look out of the window," she said softly. "Please."

Mario moved the blinds that were directly behind her. He was stunned when he saw a man standing across the street dressed in all black. "Who is that?" he closed the blinds.

Silence.

"So it's like that?" Mario asked rocking slowly like a pendulum. "You got your little boyfriend to protect you against me?" he paused. "What are you...the first lady?"

"All I want is to be happy, Mario. And if I thought it was with you I would allow that, but I realize it's not." She paused. "I use to feel badly about that. I don't anymore."

He looked down at her, tears welled in his eyes but never released. "I'm done." He walked toward the door. "When you see your boy tell him I'm going to meet him at that church tomorrow. If he got beef with me we'll put it on the line then. Let the blood fall where it may!"

And They Call Me God

THE NEXT DAY

After just leaving the church Devonte sat in the backseat as Tykisha steered the car down the highway. Although he told Lauren he would propose to Tykisha, and the ring was in his pocket ready to do the deed, he held off because of everything that was going on around him.

"Are you okay, Devonte?" she asked looking at him through the rearview mirror? "You haven't said anything in hours."

He sighed. "What do you want out of life, Tykisha?"

"To be with you." She paused. "It's the only thing I've ever wanted."

He nodded. "Outside of that. Do you have any hopes and dreams that don't include me?"

She shrugged. "It was always you, but I wanted a life with my daughter too. But if it means not having you in my life it's not worth it to me anymore."

Although it was Devonte's idea that all of his women give themselves to him exclusively, he was disappointed that she didn't fight harder for her own child. Her loyalty seemed misplaced and he didn't know if he should love or hate her for it.

"You don't have any remorse for choosing me over your daughter?"

"Not anymore," she said quickly.

Was this the woman that he wanted to be his wife? Although he was aware that if he asked, she would be a consolation wife, she wasn't ideal.

"Why you ask, God?"

"Trying to make an important decision that's all," he said pushing his shades closer to his face.

"I know it's fucked up about my daughter, and that I might seem shallow, but it has always been you." She paused. "What do you think about me?"

"I think you are a rider and I need that more than I do love."

She swallowed. "So you don't love me?"

Silence.

"Don't feel bad, Tykisha. What we have is better. When you know where a person is coming from, and love is not involved, things begin to make sense. Our setup consists of a dope man and his wife. You fit into that category and it's natural for you. Some chicks try but if she isn't bred a certain way it won't work. The difference is on a cellular level. Handling a nigga like me needs to be in the blood."

She smiled and with wide eyes asked, "You're going to make me your wife aren't you?"

The blazing sirens interrupted them as three marked police cars pulled up behind them. But Tykisha was so busy wanting to be crowned that she didn't care. "God, are you going to make me your wife?" she asked louder looking at him through the rearview mirror. "If so ask me now. I'm ready."

"Just handle the car," he said focusing on the matter at hand.

Tykisha swerved a little, not knowing what to do. "Say the word and I'll run them mothafuckas. I'm good behind the wheel."

Devonte sighed. "Don't do it." He took a deep breath and adjusted the God chain around his neck so that it sat directly in the middle of his chest. "Just...just pull over."

Obeying, Tykisha whipped the car to the left and waited patiently for the cops to approach. On queue six police officers exited their cars and surrounded the

And They Call Me God

vehicle with guns aimed. "Hands in the air," one of them yelled.

Tykisha placed her hands up followed by Devonte. When it looked safe, one police officer pulled her door open while another yanked Devonte's, dragging them both to the ground.

"Don't move!" They yelled aiming their weapons at their head. "Don't fucking move!"

Tykisha looked over at Devonte with tears rolling down her face. With her cheek pressed against the concrete she yelled, "I love you, God! I love you," she continued before he was snatched up and placed in another car.

CHAPTER FOURTEEN

PRESENT DAY

Samantha sat back in her seat in the police department and said, "That's about all I know." She crossed her legs. "I wish I could help you more."

Heidi looked closely at her again realizing something about her was off. "So who killed the people in the church?"

Suddenly Samantha laughed hysterically and Heidi and June looked at one another in confusion. "Samantha, who killed the people?" June repeated.

Samantha quieted down, reached in her purse and pulled out another cigarette. It was her last. Wiggling it she said, "Can I have one more for the road?"

June removed the lighter from her pocket and fulfilled her request so she could get rid of the bitch once and for all. "That's the last one," she said seriously, tiring of her bullshit.

Samantha took a deep pull, leaned back and released clouds into the air. "I killed them," she said softly. "Every last one of them." As if telling a horror story she grew animated. "With their eyes on Devonte I walked up behind them and put them to sleep with a slug to the back of the head. I wanted him to know that I would do whatever I could to get closer to him." She paused. "But he was scared of me and ran away where Tykisha was already waiting." She laughed. "I don't think she knew about anything either."

And They Call Me God

Nothing made sense to the detectives as they continued to listen.

"I tried to have Lauren killed on that night too, when she walked into her house alone. But Devonte was smart enough to have somebody protecting her. It was one of my friends outside of the Harrington family. But please don't tell him," she whispered as if she were a bad little girl. "If Devonte knew I had friends outside the progeny he would've never forgiven me. Our friendship had to be a secret." She paused. "But since he's gone I guess it doesn't matter anymore." She shrugged. "It's amazing what addicts will do for a hit."

Heidi and June stared at one another.

With wide eyes Heidi yelled, "Why would you kill all of those people?" When Samantha didn't respond she snatched the cigarette from her lips and smashed it on the floor. "Why did you do it?"

With a smug look on her face she leaned back and crossed her legs. "Because he was supposed to love me." She paused. "The others had a place in his heart, but he always overlooked me. It was as if I wasn't there. And ladies, there's nothing worse than needing the love of a man and not having it return."

"But you said he called you to the church that day," Heidi said. "And that when you got there others from the family were present."

"He did," she nodded. "And they were. I guess he had something else planned for us but I don't know what because I moved first. Everybody he wanted to get rid of was there except The Triad, Mario, Lauren and Tykisha. But guess what, he invited me." Her expression grew dark. "I guess it means I was expendable."

"How did you do it?" June asked, angry she didn't see this coming. "How were you able to murder all of those people?"

"Here's a hint," she winked. "I don't play guitar." She fixed her gaze on the floor. "Look inside and you'll find the answer."

Heidi turned her focus to the black case next to the table. Slowly she moved toward it. Lowering her body she popped it open, revealing an automatic assault weapon.

Samantha laughed hysterically as June rushed out to get more officers. She couldn't believe they were in the room with a madwoman, who had a loaded gun below their noses.

Quickly the officers stampeded into the room and knocked Samantha's giddy ass to the floor. Skirt up over her hips and face down on the ground, they slapped handcuffs on her wrists before pulling her out.

She laughed the entire way.

Devonte sat across from undercover female police officers June Cash, aka Rebecca and Heidi Bryant, aka Eddie. The moment he heard their voices he laughed. "Lauren was right," Devonte said softly.

"She's a smart girl," June said.

"We've been following you for awhile and finally we got your ass," Rebecca said. "With all of the games you play you have no idea how fulfilling this is."

"How so?" Devonte questioned.

"You think you are untouchable," Rebecca said. "You think you can treat people how you want and get away with it. You make your followers call you God when you are far from it."

"Who...lied on me?" Devonte asked.

"Do you mean who snitched?" June questioned.

He shrugged.

"Your father," she said. Devonte trembled with anger. Things weren't funny anymore.

"But the only thing on your mind should be how uncomfortable it will be spending the next twenty something years in prison," Heidi said. "And since you are accustomed to luxury I know this is going to be a change of pace for you. Our officers are retrieving fingerprints and evidence from that church right now. You are going down."

He smiled. "Let me ask you something, did you two really fuck each other that night, or was I just hearing things?"

June smiled. "Does it matter?"

The door opened and Debra came inside. "Detectives, I have a message for you." She looked as if she saw two ghosts.

"Be right back," June said as they both moved toward the door.

"What is it?" Heidi asked the woman.

"The church has been bombed," she paused. "And we've lost some officers," she said softly. "And all of the evidence. It happened after we removed Samantha from the property."

The two detectives felt queasy.

"Your department has been trying to find you," she replied. "They looked for you in Baltimore but you requested to have the investigations done here. At first they thought you were in the church and were dead too."

"I don't understand," Heidi said. "We picked Devonte up at the same time the stash house was due to be raided. How did he know?"

The woman looked at them. "He must've been alerted. Maybe from someone in your department." She paused. "To make things worse it looks like Devonte lured everybody to the church, knowing the bomb would go off. But when Samantha went on a killing spree and killed everyone first, the cops walked into a trap, thinking they were collecting evidence. Not knowing that the bomb was below the church."

June stepped back. "Are you telling me that, the bastard had everyone in his organization led to the church with the intentions of burning them to death?"

The woman didn't respond but her answer was enough to cause them to shiver. He was far worse than they could have imagined.

"We're still going to nail his ass," June promised. "He was involved!"

"I think that will be harder to prove," she said. "There's something else," she said. "It's about his health condition."

"Tell me!" Heidi yelled when the woman was hesitant. "Fucking tell me!"

"He could not have done this alone. Devonte Harrington is one hundred percent blind."

CHAPTER FIFTEEN

For The Love Of The Lie

Lauren pulled up to the block where the church use to sit and couldn't believe the scene. Engulfed in fire, smoke oozed from the top of the steeple and there were mounds of fire trucks and firemen in front trying to extinguish the blaze.

Lauren parked sideways, hopped out of the car and moved toward the entrance. "Mario! Devonte!" she screamed trying to make it to the doors. "Please don't be in there! Please don't!"

A burly fireman stepped to her to prevent her entrance as she tried desperately to wiggle from his embrace. "Ma'am, you can't go inside. You'll be killed."

"Get off of me," she screamed trying to fight him off. "My family is in there! My family is in there!"

"I hope that isn't true, young lady. Everyone in there is dead."

Her anger turned to emotional pain as she realized everyone she loved was gone.

Again.

Lauren rushed into her bedroom, her heart pounding wildly. "Mario! Mario! Are you in here?" She looked around although she knew he wasn't anywhere to be found. Besides, whenever he was home she could smell the scent of expensive cologne mixed with alcohol oozing from his pores.

Worried about what was happening she sat on the bed, grabbed her purse and dialed the first number she memorized…Devonte's. When Tykisha answered she was shocked. "Where is D?"

"You haven't heard?" Tykisha asked suspiciously.

"If I heard I wouldn't be asking."

Tykisha laughed, "I just got out of jail but God is still inside." she paused. "You should really move on with your life, Lauren. Devonte has already chosen me. He was going to make me his wife but the cops pulled us over before he asked."

"Tykisha, the last thing I'm thinking about is being with Devonte. I just want to make sure he's okay," she said.

"Well that's not the worst of your concerns…"

"Is it about Mario?" she asked with raised brows.

"Mario?" she repeated. "I don't know anything about him."

"Then what is it?" she asked irritated.

"It's about, Rebecca and Eddie. They were undercover cops."

"I knew it," she yelled. Lauren fell back in the bed, as her tears ran toward the back of her head.

"They were trying to get information on the drug operation so they went undercover."

"I'm so disgusted," Lauren said. "I had them bitches around me and everything. Where is Devonte now? I mean, which prison?"

"Get a pen," she said. "I'll give you all the info."

From behind the Plexiglas Lauren sat in her seat and watched the door, waiting impatiently for Devonte. When it finally swung open she was surprised at how handsome he looked in his orange jumpsuit. She was also surprised that they allowed him to maintain his dark shades.

The security guard walked Devonte up to the glass and helped him down. After raising his hands as if he were blindfolded, Devonte eventually found the handset and picked it up. "Hey, beautiful."

She smiled and wiped her grin away when she remembered she was mad with him for a multitude of reasons. "I'm worried."

"About?"

She shuffled in her seat. "Everything."

He sighed. "You know that's always been your thing. You worry even when you have someone taking care of things for you. Why put yourself through stuff like that?"

She shrugged. "I don't know." She looked down at her hand that was face down on the table. "I wish I did."

He nodded. "Why are you here?" he paused. "I thought you hated me."

"I want to know something and I need to know the truth." Her lips pressed tightly together before reopening. "Where is Mario?"

He exhaled. "I don't know, Lauren. But you should get use to not seeing him around anymore. The last I heard he moved on with his life."

Her stomach felt as if it buckled. "What...what do you mean?"

When he remained silent she realized that even if he wanted to give her the bloody details he couldn't. With the murders and bombing at the church, they were unable to pin anything on him due to his condition and a lack of evidence pointing at him. Besides, everything had been burned. And most of his conversations happened on the roof or balcony, and could not be recorded. But instead of releasing him they kept him behind bars to make sure nothing else surfaced.

The back of her throat tingled upon hearing what he said about Mario. "I loved him," she said softly. "Not as much as he wanted me to. But as hard as I could."

"I know." He paused. "And he loved you too," he cleared his throat after remembering that he had to be careful to keep things in the present not past. "I mean...he loves you."

"He would've never hurt me," she whispered. "I'm sure it wasn't him the other night."

Devonte, still unaware of Samantha's antics said, "Then who else?" he paused. "Even if he didn't, he crossed me."

For a second she stared over at him, remaining quiet. "Why didn't you want me? Why didn't you choose me when I did everything but drop to my knees?"

"Because I wanted you to have a man who could appreciate your beauty," he paused. "Even in your older years when you would need to hear it the most."

She tilted her head to the right. "I don't understand."

"I knew if you got with Mario, the only man who loved you half as much as me, that he would appreciate what it meant to be with you. And that he would tell you that everyday, since I couldn't. But he was weaker than I thought and couldn't do the job."

"But why couldn't you?" she frowned. She asked the same question before and never got an answer, so she didn't expect this time to be any different.

"Because I'm blind, Lauren."

She looked at him, preparing to laugh but his stiff stance told her he was serious. Was this some scheme in an effort to beat the charges? And did she need to play along?

"But how?" she paused. "I've seen you walk around without canes. You move around your apartment like it's nothing."

"When I'm familiar with a place I count the spaces, sometimes not even needing to do that if I memorize it. If I'm not familiar with the place I click my tongue and the echo back lets me know where something is. It's called human echolocation. If I don't do the noises The Triad helps me around. If you think back, they are always with me or near."

"So they know?"

"Yes," he nodded. "They're the only ones who do. And they've kept my secret."

"But why hide it? I don't understand."

"Because of my profession, Lauren. Blindness may be seen as a weakness."

"So...so you've never seen me?" She placed her hand over her heart.

"No," he whispered. "Although I wish I had, baby," he exhaled. "So much."

"So how do you know I'm beautiful?"

"I had Greco describe you to me in great detail." He said passionately. "He has been a fan of yours from the beginning so nobody does it better."

Her body collapsed forward and she placed her elbows on the desk. "I'm so confused."

By T. Styles   219

"Don't be. When you're blind your other senses are heightened. The sense of touch, smell, taste, hearing...but I can also feel your energy. I felt you cared about me even before you said it, and it made me want to do more for you."

She sat up straight. "But I don't believe you," she said harshly. "You don't hesitate when you move. You just go. You can't be blind."

"I'm one hundred percent blind, Lauren." He paused. "I would never lie about something like that. And I would never do that to you."

Silence.

"What about when you were younger?"

He sighed. "My eyesight started leaving me as a kid. I would knock into things because I didn't understand what was happening. I didn't want to tell my aunt because she was going through too much already. With my mother and trying to pay the bills and all." He paused. "The only person I told back then was Wanda."

"Wanda?"

"The first woman I ever fucked," he shook his head. "I was a child at the time but she forced me to grow up quickly."

Lauren was flabbergasted and her tongue flopped around in her mouth. Such a large weakness on a powerful man made her even more attracted to him. Perhaps she sensed that when she first met him.

"Don't feel sorry for me," he said seriously. "That would hurt more than you realize." He leaned back in his seat. "Just because I can't use my eyes doesn't mean I'm not a man." He paused. "Anyway when I was in Dove's Home For Boys, I was locked up by myself for awhile. Even though I had a little sight at the time, it was leaving and I would close my eyes and really

And They Call Me God

practice echolocation. I would walk around the room, click my tongue and I would faintly hear the echoes bouncing off of objects and would know how close they were. I can't explain it."

"Do you even know why you're blind?" she asked.

"I got my eyes checked once in Dove's Home and they said I had glaucoma. It wasn't bad at first. Things seemed cloudy and if I tried hard I could do all right but through the years it worsened. Maybe I didn't want to see life in the same way anymore so I lost my vision." He paused. "Before I didn't care much but that was before you."

"What do you mean?"

"I've done a lot of terrible shit in my life and this is my punishment. Never being able to see the woman I love, and the only woman who sincerely loved me back."

Lauren placed her hand over her mouth and suffocated a sob.

"Why you crying?" he asked.

Shocked she moved her hand slowly and asked, "How did you know?"

"I told you I can feel you."

She observed him quietly, hating herself for loving him despite being aware that he killed Mario. She exhaled and asked, "When are you leaving?"

"Any day now," he paused. "They have nothing on me. They have to let me go. I'm just waiting on my lawyer to give the word."

She nodded. "When you get out of here I will tell you how I feel about you treating me so shallowly."

"What are you talking about?"

"I would not have cared if you were blind, Devonte. And I deserved that chance before you wrote me off. I hate you for denying me the love that was rightly mine and for Mario." She hung up, placed her hand on the glass and walked away.

Devonte sat in his bunk with Wakeem, one of his former soldiers who moved dope for him inside the prison. Since June and Heidi put the word out that Devonte was blind, he knew he needed to get out of prison before someone tried to get famous on his name.

"I spoke to Chicago's girlfriend on a face to face visit earlier today," he said. "They told me to tell you it was taken care of."

Devonte walked away from him, counting fifteen steps out, he leaned against the wall. "Did she say how...did she say how it was done?" he stuttered.

"No. Just that it was quick."

THE MORNING AFTER MARIO LAST SAW LAUREN

Sitting in one of the pews in Devonte's church, Mario looked up at Jesus who was nailed to the cross. With a bottle of vodka in his hand and a gun on his hip, he wept harder than he ever had in his life. He wept for loving a woman who would never love him back. He wept for Varro who he killed to prove he was not afraid to be tough like he thought Lauren wanted. And finally he wept for killing his cousin.

A funny thing happened after he finished crying. Staring up at the cross, his heart open wide, his emotions on a roller coaster, for the first time in a long time he felt relief. It was time to put his life back together and move on.

First he was going to tell Lauren that he loved her and that he was wrong for trying to control her. Afterwards the plan was to let her go, holding on to a woman who didn't want him was futile and a waste of time.

He also made up in his mind that he was out of the Harrington family and would leave his beef with Devonte behind. He didn't know what life had for him in terms of a career, but with a little money saved up he hoped it would come to him real soon.

Pulling himself together, he stumbled out of the church. But the moment he hit the sidewalk he was surprised when Chicago pulled up in an all black van. "You gotta come with us, it's Lauren!" he said holding the door open. "I think she's hurt."

Inebriated and not thinking straight, Mario hopped in the van. Once inside, when he saw Shaw and Greco his heart started rocking. He was within the jaws of death. "Where is she?" he asked.

"Don't worry," Greco said handing him a bottle of vodka. "Get this up in you so you can relax." He paused. "We'll take you to see her later."

Mario twisted the top off, downed as much as he could swallow before doing it again. When he was done he handed the bottle back to Greco. Although he was drunk his senses were in tact and he knew the inevitable was about to happen. "I'm not going to see her am I?" he asked.

"No, man," Greco said softly.

By T. Styles

"Is she hurt?"

"No," he said confidently. "She's fine."

Mario shook his head and laughed. "After all this time he's finally going to do it. He's finally going to kill me."

"We're sorry, man," Shaw said. "But we think you snitched and told the cops that we moved dope out of the church."

They were unaware that Devonte's father had been involved. His father learned that a dope boy with the same last name set up shop in a little church and to avoid scandal he sold him out.

"You never wanted no parts of the church anyway," Shaw added. "Telling the boys in blue was just your way of seeing that it was over."

"I'm not gonna lie, I'm not with moving drugs out of a church. But I swear on what's left of my life, that I didn't tell the cops. I'm a lot of things...a snitch ain't one of them."

"Sorry, brother, wish I could believe you." Greco raised his arm, tugged the trigger and killed Mario on the spot.

When he was slumped over, he fired multiple bullets into his chest cavity for good measure.

Devonte was over his grandmother's apartment after being released from prison two weeks earlier. With all of the witnesses being eliminated the state didn't have a case so they had to let him go.

He wasn't foolish though. A lot of blue blood bled in that church and he knew the cops were watching his every move. He was done with the dope game…for the moment anyway. He saved up enough money to buy Lauren a ranch in Texas, complete with horses and everything she needed to take care of them.

Cleaning up loose ends, last night he told Tykisha that he couldn't be with her. She took it so hard he sent Chicago over his apartment, where they lived, to make sure she wouldn't kill herself. And the last time he called, Chicago said she was sleeping.

Mentally drained and ready to get away, Devonte grabbed a bottle of beer out of the refrigerator and sat at the table to drink it. When he was done the door opened and Lauren came inside, "You ready?"

He grinned. "I am if you are."

Nestled in the sunlight, Lauren rode down the street in her red drop top Mercedes Benz, as Devonte leaned back in the passenger seat, his right foot hiked on the dashboard. Every so often a twinkle of the sunlight would flirt with his GOD medallion, causing the diamonds to sparkle.

Devonte exhaled and said, "I want to ask you to be my wife, but I'm not going to do it right now."

She laughed and placed her hair behind her ear. "Good, because I don't know if I would say yes anyway."

He grinned. "You would." He said confidently. "I've been the nigga for you from the gate." He paused. "I'm just glad you finally realized it."

She couldn't get over his cockiness but it was one of the reasons she loved him so much. Part of her soul felt guilty for feeling free to love him, considering what was done to Mario. But she was a dope man's wife, with or without a ring. And death was always on the addendum in the drug game.

Devonte turned his head to the right so that the sun could wash his troubles away. And yet, deep down he felt like this was not his life. Was he the type of nigga who got to run away in the sunset with the bitch of his dreams? Or was he the kind who fell victim to the streets, flesh open, face down in his own blood?

"If we were to be married, tell me how our life would be," he said.

She grinned. "So now you want me to tell you a bedtime story?" she joked.

"Humor me," he laughed.

"Okay, well I imagine we would live on a big ranch. And before you get all crazy understand that ranches are beautiful."

"What if I told you I bought you one already?" he asked.

Her eyes expanded.

"Where do you think we're going?" he continued.

"You said on a road trip to Texas."

"I don't do road trips," he said confidently. "I make moves." He paused. "The ranch is yours and that's where we're going now." He winked. "Now finish telling me."

She tried to calm down but the excitement he caused made her feel bubbly. It was hard to concentrate let alone talk. It wasn't the materialistic things that made her so grateful even though she appreciated nice things. It was because he was putting a real effort to sharing a life with her. The life of her dreams.

"Well, we'd have plenty of horses and I'll even teach you how to ride one." As she spoke, she really pictured their lives together and Devonte did too. "We would have two kids, a maid once a week, and we would be helplessly and happily in love."

He nodded. "You could be with a nigga like me?" he asked. "A man who can't see?"

"For life," she said confidently, staring contently at him even though he couldn't see her.

"I didn't tell my aunt I forgive her," he said softly. "If something were to ever happen to me, can you tell her that?"

Her stomach flipped. "Don't talk like that, Devonte. You make it sound like you expect something to happen."

"No," he said. "We are going to have the life we planned. Its just that she is on her dying bed and I finally understand how it feels to have forgiveness." He paused. "You taught me." He continued. "And for the first time in my life I have the kind of peace that I would want everybody to have."

"Okay, baby," she smiled although not wanting too. "I will."

She stopped at a stoplight. Suddenly a beautiful silver Chrysler pulled up on the right side of the car and a pretty girl with the blondest hair she'd ever seen smiled at her. She realized in that moment she had albinism but it didn't take away from her beauty.

"I love you, Lauren," Devonte said as if sensing that something was off.

"I love you too," she said. "Always have and always will."

Lauren waved at the girl who waved back with a hail of bullets aimed at Devonte's upper and lower torso. She screamed in horror, as she witnessed the man she was in love with exploding into a pile of guts and blood before her eyes.

With Stanford's last wish being carried out, Ninny drove away from the scene, leaving Lauren alone and broken hearted.

And They Call Me God

By T. Styles 229

CARTEL PUBLICATIONS
PRESENTS

The Cartel Publications Order Form
www.thecartelpublications.com
Inmates **ONLY** receive novels for $10.00 per book.
(Mail Order **MUST** come from inmate directly to receive discount)

Shyt List 1	_____	$15.00
Shyt List 2	_____	$15.00
Shyt List 3	_____	$15.00
Shyt List 4	_____	$15.00
Shyt List 5	_____	$15.00
Pitbulls In A Skirt	_____	$15.00
Pitbulls In A Skirt 2	_____	$15.00
Pitbulls In A Skirt 3	_____	$15.00
Pitbulls In A Skirt 4	_____	$15.00
Victoria's Secret	_____	$15.00
Poison 1	_____	$15.00
Poison 2	_____	$15.00
Hell Razor Honeys	_____	$15.00
Hell Razor Honeys 2	_____	$15.00
A Hustler's Son 2	_____	$15.00
Black and Ugly As Ever	_____	$15.00
Year Of The Crackmom	_____	$15.00
Deadheads	_____	$15.00
The Face That Launched A	_____	$15.00
Thousand Bullets		
The Unusual Suspects	_____	$15.00
Miss Wayne & The Queens of DC	_____	$15.00
Paid In Blood (eBook Only)	_____	$15.00
Raunchy	_____	$15.00
Raunchy 2	_____	$15.00
Raunchy 3	_____	$15.00
Mad Maxxx	_____	$15.00
Quita's Dayscare Center	_____	$15.00
Quita's Dayscare Center 2	_____	$15.00
Pretty Kings	_____	$15.00
Pretty Kings 2	_____	$15.00
Pretty Kings 3	_____	$15.00
Silence Of The Nine	_____	$15.00
Silence Of The Nine 2	_____	$15.00
Prison Throne	_____	$15.00
Drunk & Hot Girls	_____	$15.00
Hersband Material	_____	$15.00
The End: How To Write A	_____	$15.00
Bestselling Novel In 30 Days (Non-Fiction Guide)		

And They Call Me God

Upscale Kittens	_____	$15.00
Wake & Bake Boys	_____	$15.00
Young & Dumb	_____	$15.00
Young & Dumb 2:	_____	$15.00
Tranny 911	_____	$15.00
Tranny 911: Dixie's Rise	_____	$15.00
First Comes Love, Then Comes Murder	_____	$15.00
Luxury Tax	_____	$15.00
The Lying King	_____	$15.00
Crazy Kind Of Love	_____	$15.00
And They Call Me God	_____	$15.00

Please add $4.00 **PER BOOK** for shipping and handling.

The Cartel Publications * P.O. BOX 486 OWINGS MILLS MD 21117

Name: _____
Address: _____
City/State: _____
Contact# & Email:
_____

Please allow 5-7 BUSINESS days before shipping. The Cartel is NOT responsible for prison orders rejected.

NO PERSONAL CHECKS ACCEPTED

CPSIA information can be obtained at www.ICGtesting.com
Printed in the USA
LVOW08s0423280516

490348LV00002BA/181/P